Unbuttoning
the CEO

Unbuttoning the CEO

MIA SOSA

FOREVER
YOURS

New York   Boston

Copyright © 2015 by Mia Sosa
Excerpt from THE SUIT'S UNDONE #2 copyright © 2015 by Mia Sosa
Cover design by Elizabeth Turner
Photography by Shutterstock
Cover copyright © 2015 by Hachette Book Group, Inc.

Forever Yours
Hachette Book Group
1290 Avenue of the Americas
New York, NY 10104
hachettebookgroup.com
twitter.com/foreverromance

First edition: December 2015]

Forever Yours is an imprint of Grand Central Publishing.
The Forever Yours name and logo are trademarks of Hachette Book Group, Inc.

The Hachette Speakers Bureau provides a wide range of authors for speaking events. To find out more, go to www.hachettespeakersbureau.com or call (866) 376-6591.

The publisher is not responsible for websites (or their content) that are not owned by the publisher.

ISBN: 978-1-4555-6841-3

This book is dedicated to my amazing husband. Thank you for laughing at the right moments, listening to my rants, and loving me always. I adore you.

Acknowledgments

It's hard to believe I've reached the point in my writing career when I have to pen my first acknowledgments. I get teary-eyed just thinking about it, so I've poured myself a hefty glass of wine to fortify me. Here I go.

To my husband: Dedicating this book to you is not enough to show my gratitude for your unwavering support and encouragement. You've helped me to live my dreams, and you didn't blink when I chose to reinvent them. *Te amo.*

To my daughters: Mommy knows her new career has changed your lives, too; thank you for adapting to those changes in stride. Every hug, every pat on the back, and every question about my writing life means more to me than words could ever say. We each could pretend we love the other more, but I'm content to call us even. Close the book now, okay?

To my mother: It was not until I had my own children that

I realized what a special mother *I* have. I owe you so much, it's hard to fathom I'll ever be able to repay you. I'm working on it, though. *Beijos, Mãe!*

To my critique partner and friend, Olivia Dade: You pushed me when I needed to be pushed, and treated me like a delicate flower when I was vulnerable and needy. I can't imagine what the last year of my life would have been like without you in it. *We did it, lady!*

To my editor, Dana Hamilton: After our first conversation, I concluded that we'd work well together, but I had no idea that we'd have so much fun, or that you'd champion my manuscript in the way you did. I'm so glad you have my back, and I look forward to more fun times ahead.

To my agent, Sarah Younger: I can't definitively say that fate brought us together, though I suspect that's the case. I *can* definitely say, however, that I am so fortunate to be working with you. I appreciate your smart advice, your effective advocacy on my behalf, and your hilarious gifs.

To the Dragonflies: I'm so proud to call you my friends. Thanks for answering the Dragonfly call, no questions asked.

To MY: You'll always have a special place in my heart. I'm so lucky to have you in my life.

To my *Hermanas*: Whether near or far, each of you is always with me.

To the Forever Yours team at Grand Central Publishing: Thank you for welcoming me to the family and for every effort you've made to get my manuscript into the hands of readers.

This required more than one glass of wine, by the way.

Unbuttoning
the CEO

CHAPTER ONE

Ethan Hill couldn't have imagined a more craptastic morning.

He stood next to his lawyer in a dim and musty courtroom in the nation's capital. The dreary atmosphere made his stomach churn. And the gluten-free muffin his assistant had given him earlier wasn't helping matters. Now that he thought about it, what the hell was wrong with gluten anyway?

Judge Monroe, a regal woman with a crop of silver hair and flawless skin, peered at him over her tortoiseshell-framed glasses and cleared her throat. "Mr. Hill, as I'm sure you're aware, a reckless driving conviction carries the possibility of a one-year jail sentence. It's not my penalty of choice, but given that you've accumulated five speeding tickets in as many months, a fine won't do."

Jail? Was she seriously considering jail? Ethan's heart raced, and his knees threatened to buckle. He even considered running through the Lamaze breathing his sister Emily had practiced in preparation for the birth of his niece. *Hee-hee-hooo. Hee-hee-hooo.*

Judge Monroe clasped her hands and leaned forward. "Your company's support of charities is to be commended. But in my view, a man who claims such *devotion* to charitable endeavors ought to spend time serving the community rather than throwing money at it. I'm sentencing you to community service."

Ethan's heart slowed to a gallop. Given a choice between jail and a couple of weeks of community service, he'd pick community service any day. "Thank you, Judge Monroe."

"Hold on, Mr. Hill. You might not want to thank me just yet."

Ethan's stomach twisted, ending its protest with a loud gurgle. *Damn you, gluten-free muffin.*

Judge Monroe scribbled on a legal pad. Ethan couldn't see what she wrote, but the hard strokes of her pen suggested she wanted to stick a figurative foot up his butt. Ethan mentally prepared himself to bend over.

After a few seconds, the judge looked up and smirked. Or was that a snort? Dammit, he wasn't sure.

"Mr. Hill, I'm sentencing you to two hundred hours of community service, to be completed with one charitable organization over the course of the next six months. Choose a charity that could benefit from your technical skills. And have your lawyer inform my clerk of the charity you've selected."

Ethan swiped a hand down his face. The sentence was outrageous. He calculated the hours in his head, figuring he'd have to spend just under eight hours a week for the next twenty-six weeks to fulfill the sentence. He doubted he could manage to do that on top of his eighty-hour workweek, but he didn't appear to have a choice.

His lawyer, a buddy from college with stellar credentials and a ruddy, cherubic face, leaned his stocky frame toward Ethan and whispered in his ear. "You got off easy, pal. Judge Monroe tends to take creativity to a new level when she's pissed. She must have gotten laid last night."

Ethan's gaze darted to the judge, whose tight expression made him wonder whether she'd heard his lawyer's quip. He'd dealt with intimidating businessmen twice her size, but when her bespectacled gaze landed on his face, Ethan barely suppressed the urge to squirm.

She took a deep breath. "Mr. Hill, use this sentence as an opportunity to think about your choices. Self-destructive behavior is one thing. Behavior that endangers others is quite another. And be prepared to take the bus for the next several months. What you do after that is up to you, but if you get another speeding ticket, this court will impose the maximum penalty. Got it?"

"Got it, Your Honor."

Judge Monroe nodded. "Court is adjourned."

The slam of her gavel against the bench might as well have been a slap upside his head. As he watched the judge exit the courtroom, Ethan vowed never to speed again. He couldn't afford to go to jail. Not again anyway.

* * *

Back at the office, Ethan's first task was to update the company's board about his legal situation. Two years ago, the board had taken a chance on him. He'd be wise not to alienate any of its members, especially when those members had hired him based on his vow that his reckless days were over.

He'd just begun to type an e-mail to the board when Mark Lansing, the company's CFO, waltzed into his office. Mark also served as his personal pain in the ass. And though he hesitated to tell Mark this, Ethan considered the man his best friend.

"Well, well," Mark said. "If it isn't Dale Earnhardt, Jr., in the flesh."

"Very funny. This time, I'm screwed."

Mark rubbed his hands together as he sat down. He didn't bother to hide his wide grin. "What happened?"

"She gave me community service. Two hundred hours of it."

Mark scrunched his brows and whistled. "That's harsh."

"Harsh or not, the sentence stands."

"How long do you have?"

"Six months. I get to pick the organization, but it has to be the right fit for my technical skills, whatever that means. And I'm going to use my first name there."

He hadn't used his first name since he'd left home to attend college at Penn. Sure, he wasn't a household name, but thanks to Google, anyone could easily discover his role in the corporation. If all went according to plan, no one at the organization would know he was the CEO of a multimillion-dollar communications company. And no one would know about his unflattering past. *How refreshing.*

Mark tapped his lips with a single finger. "And by first name, do you mean you plan to go in under the radar?"

Exactly. If no one knew who he was, the board could pretend it never happened. "Right. Something on your mind, Mark?"

Mark's gaze shifted around the room as he tapped his hands on Ethan's desk. His eyes were bright. Too bright. "Give me a minute. I'll be right back." Before Ethan could stop him, Mark shot out of the chair and left the office.

Ethan turned back to his computer. He'd just finished the e-mail to the board when Mark returned and dropped a section of the day's newspaper on his desk.

"Check that out," Mark said.

Ethan sighed, the steady throb at his temples making him more irritable than usual. "What am I looking for?"

"C-2. Flip the page."

Ethan turned the page. The headline of the full-page article read, LEARN TO NET TEACHES STUDENTS AND SENIORS HOW TO SURF THE WEB.

A photograph of a woman and two young boys accompanied the article. The boys sat in front of a computer and the woman stood behind them, her arms draped over their shoulders. Her dark, wavy hair fell against her cheeks, and her brown eyes gleamed with excitement. He scanned the first paragraph, searching for her name.

Graciela Ramirez.

A dozen images hit him at once. All of them involved Ms. Ramirez in a compromising position. With him. He looked up at Mark, who studied his reaction to the photograph. Ethan shrugged and tossed the newspaper on the ever-increasing pile of untouched papers on his desk. "I'll read it later. I need to get this e-mail out to the board."

Mark smirked. "Okay, sure. It's too bad, though."

"What's too bad?"

"She's engaged."

If he'd had a gun pointed to his head, Ethan would have been hard-pressed to explain why he was disappointed by that knowledge. "How do you know?"

Mark smiled. "It says so in the article you're going to read as soon as I leave." With his smile still in place, Mark sauntered through the door and saluted Ethan before he closed it.

When the door clicked shut, Ethan dove for the paper and placed the page in front of him. According to the article, Ms. Ramirez had been promoted from program manager to director three months ago.

The mission of Learn to Net—or LTN, as she referred to it in the article—was to serve individuals without regular access to computers, educating them about online research libraries, online job applications, social media websites, and other resources on the Web.

He read further, looking for information about Ms. Ramirez's engagement. Finding none, he gritted his teeth, speed-dialed Mark, and placed the phone in speaker mode.

Mark answered after the first ring. "What?"

"It doesn't say she's engaged."

Mark chuckled. "No, it doesn't. But you'd only know that if you read the entire article in the few minutes since I left your office. You're so predictable that I can predict when you're trying not to be predictable."

"Is she engaged or not?"

"I have no clue," Mark said.

"Do you know anything else about her?"

"Nope."

Ethan threw his head back against his chair. "I'm surrounded by people who are useless to me."

"You're wrong. I listen. Aren't you the man who whined about wanting to meet someone without the baggage of your pseudo-celebrity status getting in the way? Here's your chance, *Nic*."

"Your craftiness scares even me."

Mark snorted. "One day, you'll thank me. I'm hanging up now."

"No, wait."

"Is this about the company?" Mark asked.

"Yes."

"Good, because I'm not inclined to provide any more advice about your miserable love life."

"Mark, shut the hell up already. This is about the computer systems upgrade."

"What about it?"

"Where are the old computers going?"

"I don't know. The IT department handles recycling and donations."

"Have the old computers donated to Learn to Net, but arrange for them to be donated anonymously."

"I'd love to, but I can't."

"Why not?"

"No low-key donations, remember? Board policy. All charitable donations are to be publicized within an inch of their lives. The gift of corporate giving comes with shameless promotion of the company."

Of course. Ethan had recommended that policy. From a business perspective, it made sense. Now, it seemed cold. Manipulative. "I remember. Never mind."

"Anything else?"

"No, that's all," Ethan said. Then he disconnected the call.

Rather than e-mail the board, Ethan browsed LTN's website. It was a legitimate charitable organization, with locations in New York and D.C. Given his company's interests in Internet communications, Ethan's decision to complete his community service hours with the organization was a no-brainer. His choice to serve there had nothing to do with its director. *Yeah. Right.*

Ethan squeezed his stress ball, a constant companion since he'd become the company's CEO. He hoped he wouldn't regret the decision to work with LTN. The court had ordered him to serve the community. And he would. Pretending to be someone else. At an organization with an attractive woman at its helm. *What could go wrong?*

* * *

Gracie Ramirez sat at her desk and reread the letter she'd received from Nathan Dempsey, a lawyer at a prestigious law firm near DuPont Circle. Two weeks ago, she'd agreed to host a man who'd been sentenced to community service for reckless driving. Nicholas E. Hill. Sounded plain enough. Mr. Hill's lawyer had assured her that his client posed no threat to her or LTN's members, and he'd even provided a statement attesting to Mr. Hill's criminal record. According to that record, the man only possessed a lead foot, but given LTN's limited resources, she would have been crazy not to accept the free help that went along with that foot.

With her morning to-do list set, she turned to her computer to work on LTN's annual report. Her fingers hovered over the keyboard, however, and she dropped her head. She had yet to tackle the worst part—the organization's woeful lack of funding.

Uh-uh. There'd be no pity party for her. She was going to stay positive. She refused to dwell on the fact that she'd inherited a mess of an organization, one that hadn't made a serious effort to solicit donations to ensure a steady cash flow. Still, if she didn't secure funding soon, the doors of the D.C. location would close by the end of the fiscal year. And Gracie would return to New York, where her father would greet her with open arms and a smug expression.

She'd accepted failure in her love life, but failure in her professional life was *not* an option.

A rap on her door jolted her out of her thoughts. Gracie grimaced when she saw Daniel Vargas standing at the threshold. His family, like hers, lived in New York. Somehow he'd finagled his way onto LTN's board. As a result, she'd come to think of him as her father's spy.

Daniel swept into her office and assumed a stance that reminded her of a soldier at attention: feet wide apart, chest out, and hands behind his back. "*Hola, Graciela, esta todo bien?*"

"At ease, Mr. Vargas. Everything's fine. What can I do for you?"

"I was wondering if you're available for lunch."

Gracie was thankful she had a good excuse today to turn him down. "I can't, Daniel. I have someone coming in soon. For community service. I have to give him a tour of the facility and get him started on a couple of projects."

"Fine. Another time, then."

Daniel was a prominent architect in the city, and almost universally regarded as a catch. Daniel himself thought he was a catch. Just another reason she considered him an arrogant and eligible man who simply happened to draw excellent architectural plans.

Gracie opened a drawer and reached for her purse, an excuse to avoid his gaze as she turned him down for the fifth time. "Daniel, we've been over this before. It's not going to happen. I just don't think of you that way. And your role on the board presents a clear conflict of interest." She peeked at him to gauge whether any of her spiel was sinking in.

His chest caved in at her words, but then it puffed back out. "I'm a patient man, Graciela. You will come to your senses. And when you do, I'll resign from the board. It's that easy."

Gracie's mouth gaped. Did he think the casual way in which he treated his position on the board somehow endeared him to her? Not in this lifetime. "I've got a lot of work to do, Daniel. Was there anything else?"

Wise enough to take the hint, he cut a corner and pivoted toward the door. "No, no. I'll catch up with you some other time."

She waved him off, dismissing him and his perfectly styled hair.

With Daniel gone, she swiveled her chair toward her computer screen and returned to the annual report. Thirty minutes later, her office phone buzzed and the voice of her assistant, Brenda, filled the room. "Gracie, Nicholas Hill is here to see you." After that announcement, Brenda's voice lowered to a whisper. "He's hot, Gracie. I think I'm going to head to the bathroom to sort myself out."

Gracie rolled her eyes. Brenda was a smart and efficient assistant, but she had either no ability or no desire to filter her inappropriate thoughts, which meant she shared them with Gracie—often.

"I'll be right out," Gracie said.

She straightened in her chair and twisted her neck from side to side to ease the tightness in her shoulders. Checking her reflection in the mirror near her door, she licked her lips and swept her hair away from her face. Before she reached the reception area, she took a deep breath and pasted on a welcoming smile.

Brenda came into view first. Gracie resisted the urge to laugh when her assistant fanned herself. *Focus, Gracie. Focus.*

Nicholas Hill stood with his back to her, giving Gracie a few seconds to glance at her feet to be sure her hem wasn't tucked into a shoe. Distracted by her wardrobe check, she gave him her typical perfunctory greeting as she held out her hand. "Welcome, Mr. Hill. My name is Graciela Ramirez, the director of Learn to Net. Call me Gracie. It's a pleasure to meet—"

When Nicholas Hill's warm hand grasped hers, she looked up at him and her mouth stopped moving. Brenda's assessment of his appearance was trite, but Gracie had to admit the description was spot on. This man—*her ward for two hundred hours*—rendered her speechless.

Taking in the twinkle in his green eyes and the lopsided grin that emphasized his full lips, Gracie wanted to stuff him in a box, slap a bow on it, and set it under the Christmas tree. What the hell? So unlike her. And unsettling. Frankly, she needed a minute to collect herself, because he was too much to absorb at once.

"Hello, Gracie. This isn't the best of circumstances, but it's a pleasure to meet you. And call me . . ." He paused. "Call me Nic."

Nic's deep voice filled the space as his fingers lingered on hers. Her gaze dropped to their clasped hands, a joining more intimate than it should have been in this context. He snatched his hand away, maybe in recognition of that fact, and ran it through his tousled, dark brown hair. Gracie's fingers itched to touch those locks, because she knew they'd be just as soft as they promised. Returning her gaze to his face, she suppressed a sigh.

Wait. She had to remember why he was here. He was a reckless driver, and that was a bad thing. *Bad, bad, bad.* But she couldn't help wondering whether he was reckless in more pleasurable ways. *Yum, yum, yum.*

Ugh. Get it together, Gracie. He's just a man, and you're a smart, capable professional who has an important nonprofit to run, she reminded herself.

She cleared her throat and willed herself to settle down. "I'll show you around and then we can head back to my office to discuss the projects I'd like your help with. Sound good?"

"Sounds great," he said. "Lead the way."

Gracie hesitated. It was a truth universally acknowledged that a man in possession of a pair of eyes would check out a woman's butt upon meeting her. Hoping to divert him from checking out said butt, she walked beside him and pointed out the framed awards that hung on the walls.

She was sure he was no stranger to women who came undone in his presence, and she didn't want to be the latest poor soul to join them. She tried. She did. But when she closed her eyes for the briefest of moments, she imagined Nic's lips pressed against her neck as he held her in his arms. *Do not think of him in that way. Do not think of him in that way.*

Saving LTN was her highest priority. She couldn't afford to be distracted by any man. So it should have been no surprise that Nic was distraction personified. Somewhere the gods were laughing at her. Six months. She could ignore him for that long, right? *Right.*

CHAPTER TWO

Adopting a casual stance, Ethan pretended to be unaffected by meeting Gracie Ramirez in person. His head throbbed, though. Actually, both heads throbbed. The head on his shoulders struggled to remember that for these purposes he was Nicholas Hill. The head between his legs stirred awake, wanting to join the fun. This was ridiculous. Why was he acting like a teenage boy who couldn't control his urges?

News flash, his body announced: *Your teenage fantasies have come to life.*

Gracie Ramirez was spectacular, and he didn't use that word lightly. Gorgeous, beautiful, sexy. Those were easy words, words that had rolled off his tongue countless times. Gracie deserved more thought than that.

She stood about five inches below his six-foot-two frame, a statuesque goddess with curves she couldn't hide behind her business casual attire. His fingers yearned to explore every inch of her tan skin. Golden wisps weaved their way through the curtain of her dark brown hair. And that mouth. Plump and covered in a light gloss, her lips distracted him. *What was she saying?*

He shifted in his stance, hoping to camouflage his erection. Unfortunately, it had gone rogue on him, content to charge into the fray without any concern for tactics or careful maneuvers. It might as well have said, *I'm going in, partner. With or without you.* Yep. He was screwed.

Gracie waved a hand in front of his eyes. "Nic?"

He shook his head. "Yes?"

"I asked if you'd like something to drink."

"No, no. I'm fine. Please continue."

She regarded him with a tilt of her head, probably wondering if he was under the influence. "The facility is divided into four equal-sized spaces, each with ten computers," she said. "The computers were donated by Mine Suite Aeronautics, a defense software company based out of Alexandria. As you'll see, they're a bit outdated, but we make do with what we have."

"It's an impressive operation."

Her eyes brightened and her cheeks flushed. "We try." She stretched her arm out to indicate that he should enter the room to their right. "We run afternoon classes on Tuesdays and Thursdays and another class on Saturday morning," she continued. "The remaining days our clients are free to come in and use the computers to practice what they've learned during their classes, to work on school projects, or to surf the Internet."

Ethan's gaze swept the large room. The light blue walls gave the room a sense of cheeriness even though it housed only two large tables with a chair and a computer at each station. A single floor-to-ceiling window provided the room with plenty of natural sunlight. And photographs of the District's famous cherry blossoms hung on the walls. The space, so different from the austere office in which he spent most of his hours, calmed him. But under the circumstances, he didn't want to get comfortable here.

Ethan turned to Gracie. "Some of your clients are minors. Do you have any controls in place to monitor their computer use?"

"We do. We've placed Internet control software on each computer, and each client has a user name and password that limits his or her access to certain content."

Ethan nodded and she continued to the next room.

"Are you comfortable with computers?" she asked.

Ethan's stomach muscles clenched. He hated this part. The part where he downplayed his professional success. But the board's directive was simple—slip in, slip out, and move on. With that in mind, he kept his response brief. "Yes."

Hearing his one-word response, her eyes narrowed, as though she'd realized just then that he was a mystery. "Do you mind my asking what you do for a living?"

"I'm in the technology industry," he responded. "Global communications, Internet communications, applications and software. I do it all."

"I'm impressed. Are you a consultant?"

"Of sorts. I get paid to make significant decisions about computer-based systems." *That much was true.*

Gracie nodded. "The projects I have in mind might not be much of a challenge, but you'd be using your skill set to give back to the community."

"That's why I'm here."

"Great," she said with a smile. "Let's head back to my office to discuss the projects."

Ethan followed her down a narrow hall. The large, open space in front of her office contained a couch and a small desk. Pointing to the desk, she said, "That's my assistant Brenda's desk. You met her in the reception area. When she's not manning the front desk, she's here."

The smell of lilacs invaded his senses when he crossed her office's threshold. Ethan's shoulders relaxed for the first time since he'd met Gracie. As he surveyed her work space, Ethan's first impression was that she was a free spirit. The office was neat and organized, but the touches of whimsy in her décor told him she didn't take herself too seriously.

A framed reproduction of Edvard Munch's *The Scream* hung on one wall, next to a framed photograph of Gracie and a friend, both of whom imitated the tortured expression in the famous painting. Under the photograph, a handwritten caption read, *Gracie and Mimi in grad school.*

On her desk, a ceramic statue of a small frog caught his eye. The frog held a parasol while it sunbathed on a lounge chair. *Puerto Rico* was scrawled across the lounge chair. "I take it you've been there?"

She looked at the statue. "Many times, yes. My parents grew up there. I was born and raised in the States, though. What about you? Ever been?"

"A few times, actually. It's a popular location for business conferences."

He wanted to say more. He'd toured the island several times when his company had considered opening a satellite office there.

He'd fallen in love with its culture. The resilience and beauty of the forts that Spanish settlers had erected to protect the island had fascinated him. And he'd developed a minor obsession with *mofongo*, a popular dish made with fried green plaintains. But if he shared these thoughts with her, he'd undoubtedly slip and say more than was wise. Twenty minutes into the ruse, Ethan's confidence waned. Could he do this?

She gestured to the two chairs facing her desk and settled into her own chair. "Please sit."

Ethan sat and waited. And tried to control the thoughts rattling inside his brain like Ping-Pong balls. Ethan didn't like surprises. And his reaction to Gracie surprised him. Flummoxed him, really. He couldn't recall experiencing instant attraction like this with any woman in his past, including the one he'd almost married. His gaze returned to her expressive face. Her smile captivated him. Made him want to be the cause of it.

In a flash, the smile disappeared. After a brief shake of her head, she straightened in her chair. Maybe he wasn't alone in this. Maybe Gracie was affected by him, too. He sharpened his gaze, grasping for a clue that she, too, sensed the tension between them. She set her clasped hands on the desk and squared her shoulders, her eyes fixed on the papers in front of her. Quite the opposite, it seemed. This was business. *She* was all business.

"I have two projects in mind," she said. "First, and especially now that I know you're familiar with computers, I'd like you to help our clients when they come for free computer time. We only have a few volunteers, and their hours are unpredictable, so it would be great if you could hang around and answer our clients' questions or figure out a technical glitch. We don't have the resources for a full-time tech."

"Easy enough. What's the other thing?"

She wriggled in her chair and darted a glance his way, eventually returning her attention to the papers on her desk. Before she spoke, she pushed a strand of hair behind her ear. His gaze wandered to her hand, searching for a ring. He relaxed in his chair when he failed to see one. After several seconds of silence, Ethan realized she was staring at him.

Crap. He'd missed her explanation. *Very smooth, Ethan. Very smooth.* He sat up and shook his head. "I'm sorry. Coffee is essential, and I didn't have any this morning. Can you go over that explanation one more time?"

She blinked several times and started over. "LTN needs an influx of funds or it's going to shut down by the end of the fiscal year. Not in its entirety, but here in D.C. The New York facility has a steady flow of cash that's been earmarked for use by New York residents, and that money can't be used for the D.C. operation."

"What about the board? Can't it help?"

She sighed. "Our board members are busy people who don't have the time to help with finding funding sources. I was given this position in large part because I had succeeded in obtaining funds in New York. But I didn't count on all the work related to keeping this place running on a day-to-day basis. Have you ever negotiated a lease in the D.C. real estate market? It's a full-time job."

Ethan understood. "Tell me about it. Our agent—" *Shit.* He clamped down on his loose lips and cleared his throat.

She waited, and he stared. Thankfully, she broke the communication impasse. "Anyway, the board's backing is helpful, but the task of getting funds ultimately falls to me. So far, I've been focused on getting funding from foundations, but I need a Plan B."

"Is Plan B where I come in?" he asked.

"Yes. I want to go straight to the source and hit up Internet and communications companies that might be interested in supporting LTN's efforts."

Ethan sensed he wouldn't appreciate what she would say next, but he relaxed his features to hide his distress. "Okay, what do you need from me?"

"We need a list of the companies in the area that are potential sources of funding. The who, what, and why, so to speak. Nothing fancy. Just something to get me going. I'll take that information and plan a funding blitz, first with letters and then personal visits to key people. It's more administrative than anything else, but I'd like to free up some of Brenda's time to help me plan classes for the fall. I know the funding players in New York, but I've only been in Washington for three months, so I'm feeling out of my depth here."

Ethan swallowed—hard. She had no idea what she was asking of him. How could he prepare an analysis of the key players and companies and leave out the important fact that *he* was one of those key players and *his* company could be a major source of funding?

He forced a smile. "Sure, I can do that." And he wasn't going to cheat his service hours. He'd do it himself. But he'd leave his company off the list and hope for the best.

Right then, he resolved to view Gracie as a business acquaintance. So long as they kept their interactions at a professional level, his failure to disclose his role at Media Best wouldn't matter. Nevertheless, his deceit sat on his shoulders, a heavy burden that promised to make him tense when he was around her. That, coupled with his attraction to her, would make this community service stint torturous. Six months of torture—for the benefit of the company and his improved image. Maybe he should have opted for jail.

CHAPTER THREE

With a resigned sigh, Gracie stared at her watch and waited for Nic to arrive. A month ago, he'd walked into LTN and knocked Gracie on her butt. Since then, she'd tried to right herself, but she'd failed. She wished she didn't look forward to the sight of him so much, but she knew that wish wasn't going to come true.

He was a regular presence, contributing five to ten hours a week on average, and she looked forward to every minute he spent at LTN. He approached his work with good cheer, and he never complained about the sentence the court had imposed on him.

Nic was a wizard with computers, and the male students loved him. He'd developed an easy camaraderie with them, and despite his obvious computer expertise, he didn't talk down to them. One student in particular, Jason, bonded with Nic like he was the older brother Jason had always wanted.

He'd also developed a humorous rapport with a trio of elderly clients who'd dubbed themselves the "Gray Ladies." They took their identity as a unit seriously, and as a unified force they reveled in making Nic uncomfortable whenever possible. He deflected their banter by pretending he couldn't hear their comments, but his flushed face and small smile revealed that he'd heard every word. Even though she couldn't see them from where she stood, Gracie knew the Gray Ladies were waiting for him with as much anticipation as she was.

She pressed her face against the glass door and surveyed the sidewalk as far as her vision would allow. Behind her, the steady thump of Willa's cane alerted her that she wasn't alone.

"What are you standing there for, girl?" Willa asked.

The petite, dark-skinned woman had one hand on her waist and another on her cane. The least feisty of the Gray Ladies was a handful, which meant the other two were a grenade and dynamite rolled into one.

Gracie moved from the front door. "Oh, I'm waiting on a delivery from UPS. I thought it would be here by now."

"Right," Willa said. She eyed Gracie like a cat studying its next meal. "I'm on to you, sweetie. I know you're waiting on that fine hunk of man who's been gracing us with his presence these past few weeks. Get ahold of yourself."

Gracie fiddled with the collar of her blouse. "What hunk of a man? Nic?"

Willa wasn't buying it. "Yes, Nic."

"Don't be silly, Willa. Nic and I are just friends."

"And that's relevant because?"

"Because it's a fact."

Willa turned and began walking to the computer room. "Just because you're friends doesn't mean it has to stay that way."

Gracie ignored the comment and followed Willa's progress, wanting to make sure the older woman didn't slip on her way to the room. Willa's heart was strong, but her body was frail. At times, she joked that all her strength was centered in her heart and her mouth, and her heart would stop beating before her mouth ran out of words.

As Gracie pushed back Willa's chair, Ms. Rubio slapped her hand on the table to get Gracie's attention. "Where's my man?" she asked.

Gracie laughed. "Do you mean Nic? He isn't yours, you know."

Ms. Rubio sucked her teeth, sticking her fists in front of her face. "I'll fight you for him."

"Now, now, ladies," said Calliope Brill, the final member of the trio. "Show some decorum, please. Real women don't fight over men. We fight *with* men, so we can get to the makeup session."

Gracie imagined Calliope had been a siren in her earlier ears, because she still had the ability to make the senior gentlemen swoon. She guessed Calliope's hair had been blond once. Today, her strands were a lustrous mix of white and gray.

If Marilyn Monroe had lived to Calliope's age, she would have looked like Calliope. One of LTN's gentlemen clients, Mr. Crandon, certainly thought she was the equivalent of a blond bombshell. In fact, he never actually used LTN's computers. He just sat in front of one and stared at her.

"I was reading last night on my e-reader, bless that thing's heart," Calliope said. "And I was finishing a steamy novel where the heroine got into a fight with some tramp over a man, and I thought, '*Time's a wastin', young lady. Get back to the man . . . that's where the fun is. Scratch him like a cat.*'"

Gracie burst out laughing, releasing a snort that sounded like a car had backfired. And that's when Nic walked into the room.

She sobered quickly, and then she enjoyed the flare of awareness in his green eyes when his gaze landed on her. She wasn't oblivious. She was sure he found her attractive, but he didn't do anything to indicate he intended to move beyond a heated gaze.

"Well, well," Willa said. "If it isn't Superman." With mischief in her eyes, Willa leaned toward Ms. Rubio. "Able to drop ladies' unmentionables in a single bound."

Nic's face turned red. Willa was *not* an accomplished whisperer.

"Come here, young man," Calliope said. "A few of my e-reader books mention 'golden showers,' and I'm having trouble finding out what it means. I want to know what I'm missing."

Nic crossed the room and whispered in Calliope's ear. As she listened, her eyes widened and she frowned. Then she pushed him away. "Well, that's just disgusting. You young people are disturbed. Sex is simple. It's a lock and a key—insert and turn, insert and turn, and then insert and turn again until the door opens. There's no need for all those bells and whistles—and nastiness."

Nic scratched behind his ear. "I didn't say I engage in that activity. I'm just telling you what it means."

Gracie covered her face. It was time to get out of here. "I'll leave you to your work," she said. Then she scurried out of the room.

Two hours later, Nic appeared at her office door.

"All done for the evening?" she asked.

He remained near the doorway. "Yes, the Gray Ladies are long gone, and Jason is packing up his stuff. He's a good kid. Knows a lot about computers. I imagine he'd be even more knowledgeable if he had a computer of his own."

"His parents work hard, but they can't afford to purchase a computer for him. He has access to one at school, but he doesn't have one for homework, and it would take him hours to get access to one at the library."

"Yeah. I never thought about it that way. Computers are ubiquitous in my world. I take having access to one for granted."

"Sounds like this community service is having a positive impact on you already."

Nic shifted from side to side. "So, uh . . . are you heading out for the night?"

"Soon. I worked through lunch, though, so I'm going to grab something to eat first."

"Could I join you?"

Gracie stared at him. It was a simple question that held no sexual overtones whatsoever. And yet . . . Whenever Nic uttered any word unrelated to computers, Gracie absorbed it as an overture. Her wishful thinking continually defeated her common sense.

"Sure," she said. "I'll have to come back to gather my papers for the evening, but we could go to the diner on the corner. How's that sound?"

"Sounds great to me."

Nic stretched, giving Gracie a glimpse of the taut stomach hidden beneath his sweater. She didn't see much, but there had to be a six-pack under there. In fact, she was sure of it. At the mere thought, her heart raced. She needed yoga—desperately—because she was anything but calm when Nic was in the vicinity.

Jumping to her feet, Gracie grabbed the jacket draped over her chair and slung her purse over her shoulder. "Let's go, then."

She walked ahead of Nic through the dark hall leading to LTN's front door. The air surrounding them pulsed with restless energy and echoed the jumpiness coursing through her. She didn't understand her reaction to his presence, but she couldn't deny it, either. His footsteps summoned thoughts of the muscles in his powerful thighs. His steady breathing conjured images of his mouth against her ear. Dammit. She was too young for hot flashes, wasn't she?

Lost in her thoughts, she'd almost reached the front door when she remembered the alarm. Stopping abruptly at the security panel a few feet from the door, Gracie reached out to set the alarm. The unexpected move caused Nic's chest to slam into her back. His arms circled her waist to steady her. Gracie stilled, unwilling to move away for a moment. She couldn't be blamed for appreciating his touch, could she?

"Oh, gosh," she said. "Sorry. I need to set the alarm."

Nic inhaled deeply and released her. "Sure."

He shifted out of her way and Gracie set the alarm. When she motioned for him to precede her out the door, he did so without looking at her.

The diner was deserted on this pleasant day in mid-September. Now that the worst of the sweltering heat of August had passed, most Washingtonians were enjoying dinner *al fresco*. Gracie wanted something quick and gluttonous, though, and the diner served the best chocolate milkshake she'd ever tasted. Her craving for one would not be denied.

As they claimed a booth, a waitress in a crisp black-and-white uniform waved to them from behind the long counter. "Be right there, folks," she called.

The cherry red laminate crackled as they settled into their seats. The booth was fitted with a retro jukebox that promised tunes from the sixties, seventies, and eighties for just a quarter a pop.

Seconds later, their waitress, a middle-aged woman with a shock of red hair, handed them their menus. "Good evening, folks. Can I start you off with anything to drink?"

Gracie didn't have to think about it. "A chocolate milkshake, please."

"Good choice," the waitress said as she handed them their menus. A blush spread across the woman's cheeks as her gaze swept over Nic. *I know the feeling, sister.* The waitress snuck a glance at Gracie and inclined her head in Nic's direction. "And you, sir?"

"I'll have the same and a glass of water." He perused the menu and set it aside. "What's good here?" he asked Gracie.

"In truth, I come for the milkshakes. But you can't order a milkshake without also ordering a cheeseburger. That's Diner 101, right?"

"I like your way of thinking," Nic said. "I'll have whatever she's having, please."

So Gracie ordered for them both.

"You got it," the waitress said. "Be right back with your milk-shakes."

"Care to make a selection?" Gracie asked as she pointed to the jukebox.

"I'll spring for the selection, but you should make it," he said as he reached into his pocket. "What's your favorite song?"

"Easy answer. 'At Last' by Etta James."

"Excellent choice."

"Three-three-four-two," Gracie said.

Nic's eyes rounded in surprise. "Definitely a favorite, I see." He punched in the numbers.

After a pause, the music began, and Etta James's voice filled the booth. Gracie's face warmed when she listened to the words. They were beautiful. But maybe this wasn't the right song to play in a small booth with a man she didn't know very well. One she was clearly attracted to. Would he think she was fantasizing about him? Oh, God, he probably did. She wanted to dive under the table to hide her embarrassment.

Nic simply watched her. The ghost of a smile hinted at his amusement, but then his face fell, and Gracie wondered where his thoughts had led him.

The waitress, with two milkshakes in hand, hovered near their table. When the music stopped, she placed the milkshakes on the table. "Your burgers will be right out. First date, folks?"

Gracie wanted to die. Right then. No funeral. No eulogy. Just a quick, painless death and an express ticket to a beautifully decorated urn. Gracie tried to laugh it off, but she jabbered instead. "Oh, no, no, no. We're just friends. We work together. Well, not for long. He's helping me. Yeah, no." She grabbed her shake and scooped some of it with a spoon, hoping for a few seconds to recover.

Realizing her mistake, the waitress rushed off.

Nic smiled, and then his voice filled the painfully awkward void. "I've been wondering about something you told me last week."

Gracie struggled to suck the thick milkshake through the straw. "Oh?"

"Yeah. You mentioned your father. Something about him expecting you to come back to New York."

Gracie rolled her eyes. "Oh, that. Well, my father's a proponent of *machismo*. In his mind, women are meant to take care of the home. Men are meant to provide for their families. Women are ruled by their passions. Men are ruled by pragmatism. He doesn't applaud my professional aspirations. To him, they're a waste. I should have been married years ago. And I should be raising his grandbabies by now."

Nic swirled his straw through the milkshake. "That must be tough. Trying to establish yourself, knowing he doesn't approve."

Gracie shrugged. It *was* tough. But she'd never complained about her father's mind-set to anyone other than her mother and her sister. Loyalty prevented her from sharing this aspect of her family dynamic to others. Nic, however, seemed genuinely curious. And his expression held no trace of judgment.

"I'm used to it," she said after a beat. "Anyway, my mother always rolled her eyes—behind my father's back, of course—and he'd never interfere with my career choices."

"How'd you pay for college?" Nic didn't give her a chance to respond before backtracking. "Sorry. That was way too personal."

Gracie shook her head. "No, no. I don't mind. My sister, Karen, and I received scholarships. The rest we paid through student loans. Lots and lots of student loans. And despite his bluster, my dad helped when he could. He's not an ogre. Just a tad old-fashioned."

"My guess is he's secretly proud of you. I don't know any man who wouldn't be. You've accomplished a lot in a short time."

Gracie basked in his admiration. A compliment about her

looks? *No, thank you.* A compliment about her accomplishments? *Yes, please.* "My father's right about a few things, though. I want a simple life. A job I love. Two or three kids. And I'd love to come home to a husband who'd cook for me. Someday."

Nic frowned, and Gracie again wished to dive under the table. What the hell was wrong with her? "Oh, gosh," she sputtered. "Listen to me. I'm talking way too much." Her face burned from the embarrassment. *Abort, abort, abort,* she told herself. "So, I know you mentioned you grew up in Pennsylvania. Siblings?"

"One. A sister. Her name's Emily. We call her Em."

"Are you close?"

"Very." His head dropped a fraction. Nothing overt, but she could tell by the set of his shoulders that something about their relationship bothered him.

"Do you see each other often?" she asked.

"Unfortunately, no. Not since I moved out here. She's settled in Pennsylvania. Has a husband who adores her. And a crazily advanced toddler who happens to be the cutest baby I've ever seen. I see them for the holidays, when I can get away. But it's not enough. And I missed Sophie's birth."

"Sophie. Is that your niece?"

"Yeah."

"And your parents?"

He didn't answer, and Gracie wondered if she'd asked one question too many. The planes of his face were etched with tension.

Finally, he broke the silence. "My parents are hardworking people. They've always wanted me to have what they didn't. Opportunities. A chance at a better life."

"And you have that?" Gracie asked.

"I do," he said.

Gracie caught the hesitation in his voice. Two definitive words wrapped in a cloud of doubt. This man's layers fascinated her, and she could spend all evening trying to peel them away, but judging from his tight expression, it was time to change the subject. "What brought you to D.C.?"

Leaning against the booth, Nic repeatedly tapped the table with both hands. "It was happenstance. The right opportunity at the right time. I knew I wouldn't stay in Pennsylvania, but I had no idea where to go. After college, I was recruited by a computer consulting firm in New York. That didn't work out, so I decided to give D.C. a try." He leaned forward to sip more of his shake.

When the waitress arrived with their food, Nic lifted his head. After giving the waitress a polite nod, he rubbed his hands together, welcoming his meal in earnest. So he didn't like talking about himself. *Interesting.*

Gracie bit into her cheeseburger and moaned. "So good," she murmured.

Nic stared at her face. Then he zeroed in on her lips.

"What?" Gracie asked. "Do I have ketchup on my face?"

Nic leaned toward her and swiped his thumb over her bottom lip. "Nope. But I wanted to do that anyway."

Gracie wanted to suck his finger. Instead, her gaze fell to her plate.

"Sorry," Nic said. "That was *not* smooth."

"It's okay. I just—"

"No need to explain. I was out of line. It won't happen again."

Gracie searched for something to ease the tension, but she came up empty. So she sighed instead. "Let's forget about it. Deal?"

"Deal," he said. Then he grabbed his burger and began eating it with comical enthusiasm. "Damn, that's good. You were right."

"Told you so," Gracie said as she wiped her chin with a napkin.

They chatted about LTN and the Gray Ladies for the remainder of the meal. After that, they each paid for their respective portions of the bill.

"I'll walk you back to the office," Nic offered. "I need to grab my bag."

"All right. Thanks."

They walked the half block in companionable silence. Just before they reached LTN's door, Nic's cell phone rang. Gracie wasn't surprised. Over the past month, the ring of his cell phone had become commonplace, just like the grimace that distorted his face when he was called away to deal with an emergency.

After unlocking LTN's door, Gracie veered toward her office while Nic headed to one of the workrooms with his cell phone against his ear. "Come and see me before you go," she called behind her. "I'll need to lock the door behind you."

"Sure," he said.

When Gracie returned to her office, she closed the door and collapsed onto her chair. Nic unsettled her, which made the simple act of having dinner with him an exhausting exercise. Her attraction to him didn't surprise her. After all, he was a handsome man. But Gracie knew better than to be charmed by good looks and a smile. What sounded the alarms in her brain was the fact that he listened to her. And he seemed genuinely interested in what she had to say. He engaged her on an intellectual level, which made him hard to resist.

Gracie had no choice but to resist him, though. She'd welcomed a man into her life once, and the results had had been ugly. When it came to men, her new manifesto was simple: *Don't let them distract you, don't expect much, and engage on your terms.* With LTN's future riding on her shoulders, she needed to abide by that manifesto more than ever.

She saw the blinking light on her phone indicating that she'd missed a call. She hit the message button and listened: "Gracie, this is Robert Banks. I'm calling to give you a heads-up that the Onyx Foundation will not be able to renew its funding commitment for the next fiscal year. The foundation itself has fallen on hard times and has a lot less money to go around. The director wants us to reapply next year, but for now it's a 'no.' I know it's disappointing, but we'll work this out somehow. Talk to you soon."

Robert Banks was a dedicated member of the LTN board. Until now, the Onyx Foundation had been a consistent supporter.

Gracie's head pounded, and she slumped her shoulders in defeat. LTN's Washington facility was on its last legs. If it failed, she'd have to return to New York, with a sign of defeat taped to her back. She'd given the board hope. Had told the board she'd devote all of her energy into reviving the D.C. facility. But so far, her energy hadn't produced results. And she was running out of time. A single tear dropped to her desk.

Hearing a knock on her door, she wiped her face and schooled her features.

"Come in."

CHAPTER FOUR

Ethan opened Gracie's office door, and what he saw startled him. Gracie sat in her chair, her back straight as an ironing board. Her eyes glistened. He'd never seen anything other than a cheerful or befuddled look on her face, so her tense expression did something to him.

For weeks, he'd suppressed the urge to pursue her, and he'd done so by erecting a wall between them. By thinking of her as nothing more than the friendly director of the organization where he was completing his community service. He'd breached that wall tonight, when he'd asked her to dinner, when he'd swiped his thumb across her lip, and when he'd asked her about her family. Ethan was on a roll apparently.

During dinner, she'd described her ideal future. And it bore no resemblance to the life he could give her. He suspected Gracie wouldn't be interested in hanging on the arm of a CEO who was invited to every ball, gala, and fund-raiser known to man. Granted, he hated the hoopla, but it was a necessary evil of his position. She was looking for a simple guy. He was anything but. So his resolve to avoid a romantic entanglement with her had solidified as they'd sat across from each other in the diner.

Now he wasn't sure of anything. Seeing her in a vulnerable state reminded him that she was a woman with a life outside these walls, and picturing her outside these walls led to dangerous thoughts. *Suck it up, Hill, and find out what's wrong.* "Is everything okay?"

"We've just lost another source of funding," she said. "The situation is getting bleaker by the minute. I'm just frustrated. It'll pass."

She bowed her head and placed her fingers at her temples.

Although he wished to, he knew better than to ask the board to help. The board wanted Ethan to serve his sentence quietly. A donation to LTN—which, under the company's policy, couldn't be made anonymously—surely would undermine that goal.

Plus, he wasn't ready to reveal who he was. If Media Best gave LTN money, Gracie would look up the company and learn he was its CEO. Ethan liked the way she looked at him now. That would change once she knew who he was.

After he finished his community service hours, he'd figure out a way to help her. For now, though, he'd do what she asked of him. He stepped closer to her desk. "I've got something that might help."

Her head whipped up. "You do?"

Ethan was drawn to the hope that shone in her eyes. He sat in front of her desk and gave her the sheets of paper in his hand. "This is the list of potential donors you asked me to create."

She looked down at the papers, blinking rapidly—to stem the tears, he guessed.

"It's in two parts," he continued. "The first part lists all potential donors. The second part lists donors I think are a good fit for the organization—they're techies, they're interested in education, they're interested in issues affecting seniors, and so on." As Ethan had planned, Media Best was not on the list.

She studied the list, and then she smiled. "Thanks so much, Nic. This is wonderful. I'll ask Brenda to start making information packets. I've got the letter of introduction ready to go."

"I'm glad I could help."

She set the list on her desk and sat back in her chair. "You've been incredible. I hate to admit it, but I'm glad you're a speed demon. I'm lucky to have you. Well, I don't *have* you. I mean, *LTN* is lucky to have you." She blew out a breath and rolled her eyes.

Ethan stared at her, not trusting himself to say anything. Her eyes were dark and hooded, and her chest rose in a steady tempo. He fisted his hands at his sides and leaned forward, pulled in her direction by the force of their mutual attraction. The desk was no barrier to the pull between them.

Her shoulders rose as she took a long breath. "Am I wrong in thinking you want to kiss me?"

And as soon as the question left her mouth, Gracie's eyes went round.

Ethan was surprised, too. Okay, then. No more avoiding the issue. With shaky hands, he smoothed the tops of his thighs. He could be honest about this. "I'd like to, but I'm not sure it's a good idea."

Her eyes fluttered, and then she opened them wide, waiting

for him to say more. She watched his every move, her gaze following his hands as he searched for something to do with them. Ethan wanted to hide, but somehow he knew there wasn't a place he could run to get away from this . . . thing between them.

"Are you uncomfortable with the situation?" she asked. "Because you're here to perform community service?"

That wasn't the reason, but he couldn't tell her the truth. Not yet anyway. "It's complicated, Gracie. There's a lot you don't know about me."

Her eyes widened in alarm. "You're not married, are you?"

"No, I'm not married."

"Engaged? Girlfriend? What?"

"No, no, and hard to explain. It's just . . . I can't be in a relationship right now. My choice."

She set the papers on her desk, the tremor in her hands betraying her composed demeanor. Her gaze swept over the list, and then she looked up at him. "I'm sorry. Those questions were inappropriate. Let's pretend they never came out of my mouth. Believe me, I'm not usually this forward. I just . . ."

She was torturing him. Absorbing the questions in her eyes, he suspected she really wasn't sure whether he was attracted to her. Ethan could disabuse her of that notion easily. But he wouldn't.

Ethan drove fast. He liked his women faster. Gracie was different. She didn't saunter, didn't bat her eyes, didn't lick her lips, or do any of the other things some women did to try to catch his attention. Flirting didn't appear to be in her repertoire, and that fact alone signaled danger ahead should he try to pursue her.

What's more, he considered himself an honorable man, one who wouldn't start a relationship on a foundation of lies. Sure, some assumed he was a player, but when it came to the opposite sex, he'd always been honest about his intentions. He couldn't afford to change his record now.

Despite all this, he knew his resolve wouldn't last long if he hung around. He had to get out of here. He stood and straightened his jeans. "I'm going to head out for the night." Then he turned and walked toward the door. He was on the verge of escaping, his hand on the doorknob, when her voice called out to him.

"Nic?"

He wasn't Nic. Not in his real life. And hearing her call him by that name reinforced his belief that walking out the door was the right thing to do. But he wasn't going to be rude about it, so he turned to face her. "Yeah?"

"I don't care. Whatever it is. I just—"

Her head lowered.

"What were you going to say?" he asked.

She blew out a soft breath and raised her head to the ceiling. He was sure she had no idea the move exposed her neck, enticing him to lick his way from there to her lips. She lowered her head and shook it. "Nothing. Never mind. I thought . . ."

The insecurity in her voice shattered his resolve. Propelled by his need to correct her misimpression of the situation, he strode across the room. She swiveled her chair toward him and braced her hands against the armrests, her big, brown eyes watching his progress. When he reached her, he bent to her eye level, cupped the sides of her face, and kissed her as she rose from the chair.

She stumbled into him and wrapped her arms around his waist, humming her pleasure as he deepened the kiss. Her lips were soft and warm, just as he knew they would be. Wanting more of her body on his, he shifted so he could sit on her desk and nestle her between his legs.

He maneuvered his hands under her curtain of hair and brushed his fingers along her neck. He breathed in the smell of lilacs, welcoming the onslaught of sensations overtaking him. She ran her hands along his waist and slipped them under his sweater, her soft fingers trailing a slow path across his skin. Heat spiraled from his stomach and radiated through his limbs. And soon, his erection strained against his pants. He was rock hard. Painfully hard.

She groaned when his thighs squeezed her hips. "More," she whispered.

Her voice held no pretense. Every single one of his actions did, however. She had no idea who he really was, which meant he had to stop. With regret, he dropped his hands and shifted her to the side so he could stand. Backing away with his hands in the air, he chastised himself for being so careless. "Sorry. That shouldn't have happened."

Her steady gaze held his. She wasn't even trying to tempt him. She just did. After a taut moment of silence, she licked her lips and returned to her chair. "It's okay. I understand."

Ethan barked out a laugh, and she regarded him with a dazed expression. No, she didn't understand. But he wasn't going to enlighten her. "See you next week," he said. Then he turned and walked out the door.

CHAPTER FIVE

Confused by Nic's behavior, Gracie invoked her fail-safe method for dealing with inscrutable men: She called her best friend and asked her to come over for a Girls' Night In.

But Mimi had her own issues to contend with. As she sat on Gracie's couch, her hands gestured in so many directions Gracie closed her eyes for fear of getting dizzy. "My boss is such a jerk, and it gets him off, I swear," Mimi said. "I wish I could leave my job." She finished her rant with a huff that ruffled her blond bangs.

Gracie hugged a pillow and gave her friend a knowing smile. "But you won't. You love your work."

"Yeah, everything except for having to work with him."

"Hmmm," Gracie responded. Then her thoughts turned to Nic. He wasn't a jerk. Perplexing maybe, but never a jerk.

Mimi slapped a hand on the sofa cushion. "And just yesterday, he tried to embarrass me in front of the team."

"Did he?" Gracie asked.

"Yeah. In the middle of the meeting, he walked to me, pulled me from my chair, and threw me on the table."

"Hmmm," Gracie murmured.

"And then he lifted my skirt and began feeling me up in front of everyone."

Wait. What did Mimi say? Gracie shook her head. "Hold on. Back up, back up, back up. *What* did he do?"

Mimi threw a sofa pillow at her. "I *knew* you weren't listening to me. And I guess it's only fair. I've been going on and on about Sir Jerk-a-Lot when you have more pressing matters on your mind. The floor is open. Discuss. Share. Tell Mimi your problems."

Gracie groaned and hid her face in the pillow. "There's a guy."

Mimi laughed. "There's *always* a guy."

"No, he's a *man*. Smart. Sexy. Genuinely kind to the Gray Ladies."

"What's his name?"

"Nic."

"So what's the problem?"

"I met him through LTN. He's been ordered to do two hundred hours of community service."

Mimi's eyebrows shot up in her typical *what-the-fuck* fashion. Gracie cringed. She could see how Mimi would get the wrong idea. "What did he do?" Mimi asked.

"He's a fast driver. One too many tickets."

"Okay, so he's redeemable if he learns to slow down. Don't want to get on a soapbox, but driving too fast has consequences for other people, too. But that isn't the real problem, is it?"

"No. I'm interested, but he's holding back for some reason.

And it's not because of the usual suspects. No wife, no girlfriend. I asked."

"Gay?" Mimi asked.

"I don't think so. His kiss was way too hot. He was conflicted about something, but trust me, it wasn't about his sexuality."

Mimi's eyes rounded, and she grabbed Gracie's forearm. "You *kissed* him?"

Gracie's ears warmed under Mimi's shocked appraisal. "Yes. And I practically begged him to. It was so embarrassing. But I got over the embarrassment. Very quickly. Because it was hot. So incredibly hot. Like molten-lava hot."

"Okay, okay. I get it. It was hot."

Gracie dropped her head. "But then he backed away. And now I'm with you, sitting on the couch, where I'll sit for another hour while the gallon of ice cream we ate makes its way through my body. Yuck."

Mimi smiled. "Maybe he's just skittish about commitment. They usually are."

Gracie shrugged. "Maybe."

"Back to the kiss. What did he taste like? Mint? Burritos? What?"

"What does it matter?" Gracie asked.

"Just answer the question."

Gracie thought about it. "Um, minty, but more like citrus or something fruity."

"Like gum?"

"Yes, probably."

"He planned on kissing you then."

Gracie stared at her friend. "You can tell that just by the smell of his breath?"

"The point, my innocent, is that he took the time to freshen his breath. He was *hoping* it would happen."

Gracie pinched the bridge of her nose. "That is not the kind of high-level analysis I've come to expect from you, Mimi."

Mimi waved her comment away like a pesky fly. "Men don't require high-level analysis. They eat, they sleep, they shit, they have sex. All the crap in between is meant to ensure women don't confuse them with apes. He's into you, but he doesn't want you to find out something about him. It's your job to figure out what he's hiding." Pointing to the laptop on Gracie's desk, Mimi said, "That thing-a-ma-jig called the Internet might be helpful. You're familiar with it, right?"

Gracie whacked Mimi's shoulder with the pillow she'd been smothering for the last minute. "I refuse to look him up. I'm not a stalker. Besides, I have his address and his social security number. What else do I need?"

"May I remind you that a serial killer has an address and a social security number, too?"

"Ah, but every serial killer doesn't have a letter from his lawyer confirming that he has no record of anything other than speeding tickets, right?"

"Not bad. But don't jump in without getting to know him more."

Gracie understood Mimi's concern, but since Gracie didn't intend to explore a relationship with Nic, she set that concern aside. "Don't worry. I don't plan on pursuing him. Besides, I think you're right. He's probably skittish about commitment. Forget I said anything."

"I'm your best friend, Gracie. I don't forget anything you say, except when you ask me to return something I've borrowed."

"Well, forget about this. My ass is still smarting from the last time a man bit me in the butt."

Mimi waggled her eyebrows. "Sounds kinky, my pet."

Gracie's gaze flew to the ceiling. "Gutter brain. I'm talking about Neal."

Neal. Her biggest mistake. The man who slotted women into two categories: women you marry and women you have sex with. It was bad enough to learn he'd ruled out a future with her. That had battered her pride. But when she learned he was stringing along another woman, Gracie had wished him every nonlethal venereal disease known to man. Fast-forward one year, and surprise, surprise, she was pining for a man who had no interest in her. Would she ever learn?

"Neal was a jerk," Mimi said. "And he didn't deserve you. You can't base your life decisions on a relationship that was going nowhere from the start."

"True. But I can learn from my mistakes. I need someone who's open, who knows how to communicate, who thinks I'm worth making a commitment to."

"And you'll find him," Mimi pressed. "Your special someone is out there. You just have to be willing to find him."

"You know, behind that badass exterior lurks an eternal optimist."

"If you repeat that to anyone, I'll arrange for sex toys to be delivered to your office on a daily basis. In clear packaging."

Gracie's eyes widened in disbelief. Mimi was a nutcase. "Anyway, nothing's going on between Nic and me. And I'd like to keep it that way."

"Bullshit," Mimi said.

Gracie groaned. Then she face-planted on the couch. Denial was getting her nowhere. "Bullshit is right."

* * *

The gods granted Gracie a reprieve, because Nic was a no-show the week after "the kiss." He'd left a message with Brenda, informing Gracie that he'd been called away on unexpected business. Right. He was on the run, and she couldn't blame him. Not when she'd all but thrown her panties in his face when he'd tried to warn her away. She searched her surroundings for her self-respect. She needed it back. Yesterday.

Thankfully, her younger sister Karen's impending visit distracted her from her thoughts about Nic. Karen would be staying the weekend, and Gracie was looking forward to spending time with her.

A senior at New York University, Karen planned to attend medical school after college. Her determination to do so meant she had little time for social pursuits. Gracie worried that her baby sister was *too* focused on her career, but Gracie held her tongue. Arguably, Gracie had the same problem, so she wasn't sure what she would say to Karen to convince her to change.

Gracie arrived at Union Station more than an hour before Karen's train was scheduled to arrive. She wandered the enormous station, marveling at its resemblance to a shopping mall. Small, nationally recognizable shops dotted the second level. The first level bustled with the activity of both travelers from far away and people who commuted to work from Maryland or Virginia. After a rest stop at a small coffee shop, Gracie walked to the waiting area where she would meet Karen.

She didn't wait long. Karen was among the first travelers to barrel through the double doors that led to the station platform. Karen squealed when she saw her big sister, and Gracie, who was just as excited, rushed to Karen and enveloped her in a tight embrace. "Oh, gosh, Kar. You're growing up so fast." And it was true. Her "baby sister" was a woman, and for the first time Gracie understood her father's desire to protect his girls from harm. She still didn't agree with his views, but she understood their motivation.

Karen rolled her eyes. "Gracie, stop. You sound like Mom. Now, take me to your fabulous apartment and feed me sumptuous food worthy of the goddess I am."

"Rice and beans, right?" Gracie asked with a smile. Karen was a sucker for the staple of her mother's Puerto Rican kitchen.

The corners of Karen's eyes crinkled in delight. "Of course."

Gracie grabbed Karen's bag, slung it over her shoulder, and linked arms with her sister as she led her to the taxi line.

As they waited on the long line, Gracie shared her exciting news. "I have a surprise for you."

Karen twisted her long hair into a bun as she searched Gracie's face. "You're pregnant."

Gracie choked on her laughter. "Uh, no. That would require Immaculate Conception, and I'm certain there are others more worthy of such a miracle."

"Okay, we'll talk about that sad fact later. What's the surprise?"

"We have tickets to see the Kennedy Center's production of *The Dancer*. Tomorrow night."

Karen's eyes widened with excitement. "No way."

"Yes, way."

As a teenager in New York, Gracie had spent hours wandering the most famous museums in the world: the Guggenheim, the Museum of Modern Art, and of course, the Metropolitan Museum of Art. The District had its fair share of wonderful art museums, but New York museums held a special place in her heart.

Given that she loved art, she could not miss the Kennedy Center's production of *The Dancer*, a musical based on Edgar Degas's famous painting *Little Dancer Aged Fourteen*. An LTN board member had offered her the tickets, and she'd snapped them up like a hungry crocodile. Karen, who loved the performing arts, would be the perfect "date" for the show.

"Do we get to dress up?" Karen asked as they climbed into the taxi.

"We do. First, I feed you. Then we shop."

Gracie gave the taxi driver her address, and Karen snuggled against her. "I'm so glad I'm here, Gracie. It's going to be a wonderful evening."

* * *

Gracie needed to use the restroom. As she'd anticipated, the performance captivated her senses—and undermined her ability to gauge when she'd sipped too much water. As soon as the intermission began, Gracie left her seat and sprinted out of the auditorium. Karen trailed behind her.

"Enjoying the show?" Gracie asked Karen as they waited in line.

"I am. It's incredible. I had the urge to use the restroom a half hour ago, but I didn't want to miss a second."

"I know what you mean," Gracie said as she rushed into the stall.

Minutes later, she and Karen met outside the restroom and debated whether to order wine. "I think I'll pass," Karen said.

"I'm going to order a glass. Go ahead back to your seat. No need to wait for me."

Karen nodded and walked away.

Gracie turned toward the bar, enjoying the slight twirl of the black jersey dress she'd worn for the occasion. Stepping around two middle-aged women in the middle of a warm hug, her eyes rounded when she saw a familiar figure.

Nic—waiting at the bar. *With a woman.* A beautiful woman with a slim figure and a stylish, pixie haircut. And she was a very possessive woman, if the hand grasping at Nic's waist was any indication.

Gracie's mouth dropped as she took him in. He'd replaced his signature outfit—a sweater and jeans—with a slate gray suit that hugged his broad shoulders and long legs. He'd combed his hair back, too, and the effect devastated her: Every feature on his face, from his pale green eyes to his bow-shaped lips, fought for her attention. She watched this stranger, noticing the details that had transformed him from a casually dressed computer consultant to the striking businessman before her. The starched white shirt. The red silk tie. The Italian leather shoes. To say that he cleaned up well would have been an understatement.

At first, Nic's face revealed nothing about his mood. But then he appeared inattentive and distracted, glancing between the watch at his wrist and the program in his hand. At one point, he gritted his teeth when the beauty next to him kissed his cheek.

Gracie's stomach twisted. Afraid she'd have to speak to Nic with that woman by his side, she dove behind the middle-aged women, one of whom wore an elaborate red hat that provided the camouflage Gracie needed.

The woman with the red hat leaned toward Gracie. "What is it, sweetheart?" she asked in a low voice.

"I don't want someone to see me," Gracie replied.

The other woman's eyes brightened with excitement. "Is it a man?"

"Yes, yes, a man," Gracie said. "A very handsome one. But he happens to be here with a date."

The woman straightened and searched the crowd, presumably for the handsome man in question. "Oh, the rat. We've got you covered."

And they did. Literally. The two women shifted to stand hip to hip as Gracie crouched behind them. "On three, we'll step back and walk to the auditorium doors," said Hat Lady. "One, two, three."

They shuffled backward and to the right as other patrons watched them in amusement. It took them fifty awkward steps to get Gracie to safety. When they reached the doors, Gracie scrambled inside the auditorium. Her saviors followed her.

"Thanks so much," Gracie told them as she turned around.

"No, thank you," they said in unison.

"That was fun," Hat Lady observed. "Good luck dealing with that man."

"Oh, no worries. I won't have to deal with him. There's nothing going on between us. But it would have been awkward. So, um. Yeah. Thanks again."

Hat Lady reached for Gracie's hand and patted it. Even she knew Gracie was deluding herself. "In any case, good luck," she said with solemn eyes.

But Gracie wouldn't need luck. Seeing Nic with another woman had reminded her that she knew nothing about him. And it wasn't due to a lack of trying on her part. Given this evening's events, Gracie repeated her mantra: *Don't let him distract you, don't expect much, and engage on your terms.*

In Nic's case, she'd simply keep him at arm's length and go about her business. Now, if she could just get her body to cooperate, she'd be in good shape. Actually, the Internet offered a quick fix for that. She made a mental note: *Go online and buy a vibrator.*

CHAPTER SIX

Nic stifled a groan when Calliope raised her hand. The woman was relentless. Her fourth interruption would be no different from the last. He was sure of it. They were twenty-five minutes into the half-hour workshop on social media, and Calliope had monopolized most of it. Much to his chagrin, Gracie stood at the back of the room, smiling at Calliope's antics.

"Yes, Calliope?" he asked.

Calliope smoothed her hair and peered over the computer monitor. "Tell me about selfies, Nic. Let's say I want to send a picture of myself to someone special."

Calliope turned sideways and winked at Mr. Crandon. The man's pointy ears wiggled, and his listless body perked up, ready to give the topic its full attention. Ethan worried the man would keel over if Calliope continued to verbally stimulate him.

Ethan walked to the front of the room. "Yes, you can use social media to send selfies, but you can also send selfies using your smartphone."

"Are there any restrictions on the *kinds* of selfies I can send over the Internet?" Calliope asked. "Will a provocative selfie get me in trouble with Big Brother, for example? Not nude *per se*. I'm thinking along the lines of a very sheer nightie."

Ms. Rubio and Willa snickered. Ethan, on the other hand, wanted to gag. Calliope had to be older than his mother. He'd always chosen to believe that his mother and father did not have sex. But Calliope was debunking that myth in front of his eyes. And speaking of eyes, the images that bombarded him were eye-gouge-worthy. In his head, he begged the images to go away.

"Ms. Brill, I can't give you legal advice about the kinds of selfies you're contemplating, but coincidentally, you can look up your question on the Internet before you send a selfie to someone."

Calliope nodded and began to type away.

Gracie covered her mouth and walked to the front of the room. He hadn't seen her in a week. As she strode to him, Ethan realized he missed her. But he didn't like the impersonal way she regarded him. He sensed she was pissed at him.

True, the last time they'd been together, he'd sprinted out of her office like an Olympic relay hopeful. But her neutral stare didn't suggest resignation; upon closer inspection, he saw fire in her eyes. She wanted to pummel him. He had the distinct feeling he'd unknowingly ventured into knee-to-the-groin territory.

"Good to see you, Gracie."

"Nice to see you, Nic. Thanks for running the workshop."

"Calliope was a challenge, but otherwise it was really fun."

Gracie nodded, skirted around him, and walked out the door. Ethan stood there like an idiot. Calliope cleared her throat and jerked a thumb in the direction of the door. Right. He had to go after her and find out what was going on.

She was talking to her assistant, Brenda, outside her office when he caught up with her. "May I speak with you in private?"

Gracie nodded and walked into her office. He closed the door and strode to the front of her desk. Gracie stood, too—as she flipped through a stack of papers on her desk. Her hair was fastened in a sleek ponytail, emphasizing her sultry eyes and high cheekbones.

She sighed and raised her head, donning a bored expression. "What can I do for you, Nic?"

"Is everything okay?"

She stared at him. "Everything's fine."

"Okay," he said.

"Okay," she repeated.

She wore a red dress that fit the contours of her body, and the belt at her waist fastened with a neat bow. He suspected the dress would fall open if he tugged the ends of that belt, leaving her almost bare and open to him. As usual, such thoughts convinced him it was time to back away. "Just wanted to be sure. I'll see you next week." He turned to go.

"Nic?" The tone of her voice matched that of a woman who was ready to squeeze his balls—to inflict pain, not pleasure.

"Yeah?" he asked as he placed his hand on the doorknob.

"Did you enjoy the performance this weekend? At the Kennedy Center, I mean."

Ethan turned around slowly. "Is that what this deep freeze is about? You saw me at the Kennedy Center with a woman?"

Gracie blushed. "You said there was no wife, no girlfriend."

"And I told you the truth," he replied. "I went to that performance with her to fulfill an obligation. There is no woman standing between you and me."

Gracie's shoulders slumped—just enough to alert him that his last comment upset her. "Fine," she said. "You don't owe me an explanation. And I'm sorry I even brought it up. What you do in your personal life is your business. *Obviously.*"

Ethan wanted to roar in frustration. She was right. He didn't owe her an explanation, but he wanted to give her one just the same. He couldn't bear the distrust in her eyes. Not when he knew she had other reasons to distrust him. If he went down, he wanted to go down for something he'd actually done—like lie about who he was.

The reasons he hadn't disclosed his identity were still valid. He didn't need the publicity. Had promised the board he'd keep the court sentence out of the press if he could. And frankly, he didn't know Gracie well enough to be sure she wouldn't reveal his identity to anyone else. But he was tempted to tell her anyway, just to wipe that look from her face.

"I'm sorry," Gracie whispered. "I'm letting my past experiences with men cloud my judgment. That isn't fair to you."

"What experiences?" Ethan asked.

She crossed her arms over her chest. "We're not having this conversation."

"My intro to Psych class taught me to listen for clues. You brought it up, which means you want to talk about it."

She stared at him.

"Look, I'm just trying to understand where you're coming from," he pressed.

Gracie inhaled and sat in her chair. "A year ago, before I came to D.C., I'd been dating a man. We'd been together for two years, and I thought we'd get married. I was wrong."

"He cheated?" Ethan asked.

"Surprise, surprise."

He *was* surprised. What kind of jerk cheated on a woman, let alone a special woman like Gracie? The man must have been an idiot, and Ethan was glad he was out of Gracie's life. "I'm sorry."

Gracie waved away his apology. "You didn't do anything. Apparently, I was too focused on my career. He felt neglected. Didn't think I was the homemaker he needed."

Ethan didn't know the guy, but he knew bullshit when he heard it. "That's crap. He was an asshole, plain and simple."

Gracie nodded her head in agreement. "You're right. And you did nothing wrong. It's me. I'm hypersensitive when I think I've been misled . . . especially when it comes to issues of infidelity." Then she appeared to realize the implication of her words. "I . . . uh . . . of course, I'm not suggesting we're together . . . but . . . uh . . . I thought we connected . . . and I . . . I'm going to shut up now."

Ethan didn't dare smile, but he wanted to set her at ease. "Gracie, my issues have nothing to do with another woman. I just don't have it in me to be in a committed relationship. I tried it once, and it didn't work. I can sense you're looking for something I'm not prepared to give."

"You're wrong," she said.

The steely determination in her voice surprised him. "I am?"

"Yes. I'm looking for a no-strings affair. Think you're up for it?"

It took Ethan several seconds to process her question. When

his brain cleared, the questions left his mouth in a torrent. "Wait a minute. That night at the diner. What was that bit about wanting to have a quiet life? The kids? The solid man? The guy who'd have dinner waiting for you when you came home? Was that a load of crap?"

Gracie angled her head and stared at him. "No, that wasn't a load of crap. It was the truth. But I didn't say I want that *right now*, did I? I'm a busy woman, Nic, and if you haven't noticed, I have an organization that's on the verge of collapse. I don't have time for a serious relationship right now."

He wasn't sure where she was going with this declaration, but he was curious enough to hear her out. "I'm listening."

"Look, you said a woman wasn't keeping us apart. And I assume a man isn't keeping us apart either."

She peered at him, waiting for his response.

"You're right on both counts," he said.

"Okay, then," she continued. "You don't have it in you to be in a stable relationship, and I don't have the time or inclination for a relationship, either. I know you're attracted to me." Her breath hitched. "And I can't believe I'm admitting this, but I'm lonely."

He just stood there, mouth open, a dumbfounded expression on his face, no doubt.

"Okay, if you must know, I'm horny, too," she continued. "And if we go into this knowing exactly how it'll turn out, what's the harm? We enjoy each other for as long as we want to."

Ethan stuck his hands in his back pockets and rocked on his heels. "What if one of us wants to end it sooner than the other?"

"Then we go our separate ways. No hard feelings. No drama.

In fact, if it will help, we can set a time frame on the arrangement."

Ethan couldn't believe he was considering it. Sure, the conversation wasn't all that different from the conversations he'd had with other women he dated, but every other time *he'd* been the one to initiate the conversation. "What did you have in mind? For a time frame?"

Her eyes gleamed and she stood a bit taller. "When you complete your community service hours, we're done. You want to move on, get in here and complete your service hours. You want our arrangement to last a little longer, come in every other week instead." She paused. "That is, unless I get tired of you first."

Ethan regarded the perplexing woman in front of him. He'd met her only six weeks ago, and yet he knew this wasn't her style. Gracie wanted hearth and home. But she was asking him for sex. "There's a catch. There's always a catch. What is it?"

Gracie sighed and snaked a hand around her neck. "No catch. But there are two conditions."

"Catch. Condition. Same thing."

"Are you going to risk this deal over semantics?" she asked.

"Fine. What are your *conditions*?"

"First, no one at LTN can know about it. Second, you get no special treatment on service hours. I won't sign off until you've completed your hours. With those conditions in mind, do we have a deal?"

Ethan considered her. She talked a good game, but her hand trembled as she twirled a pen in her hand. And she bit her bottom lip as she waited. He could nibble on that lip for her, the devil on his shoulder taunted.

Ethan took a step toward her. "So let me see if I understand what you're proposing. When I'm done with my service hours, we go our separate ways. No questions asked. No further contact."

"Exactly."

"And if I say no?" he asked.

"Then we carry on as before." When he said nothing, she waved a hand between them. "But I suspect this tension will need to be released eventually. And what happens then? I'll tell you. We'll prowl around each other, we'll undress each other with our eyes. Maybe I'll imagine what it would be like to have nothing but slick, naked skin between us." She tilted her head and shrugged. "Not sure where else my thoughts will lead me."

Ethan wanted to pant. His sweet Gracie played dirty. She might not have been in her element, but she was warming to the task quickly. She was a seductress with a sense of humor. And she'd zapped him of his strength to resist her. What's more, he was powerless to deny himself the opportunity to feast on her delectable body without the risk of an ugly scene when he walked away.

But he couldn't forget the lie that would always stand between them. She wouldn't know his real name. But they would agree never to see each other again. In that case, would his true identity matter?

A series of thoughts ran through his brain. He wasn't all that impressed with the man he faced in the mirror. A man who made high-level decisions when all he really wanted to do was sit in front of a computer and design software. Somewhere along the line he'd lost that man. He wanted to find him again. She offered him a way to do that—even if it was temporary.

"Let me think about it," he said.

But he knew damn well he wasn't going to turn her down.

* * *

Gracie gnawed on her lip as she watched Nic consider her proposal. What the hell had she been thinking? Sure, she'd delivered the proposal with the ease of an experienced femme fatale, but the contents of her breakfast were riding on a roller coaster inside her stomach.

The idea was perfect. Nic didn't want forever, and she didn't want forever *right now*. In fact, she questioned whether a long-term relationship was something she should aspire to anyway. If she didn't expect forever, she wouldn't be disappointed when it failed to materialize. Problem solved. Now all she had to do was stay focused on LTN and keep a check on her emotions as she embarked on a tawdry affair with Nic. Well, she hoped it would be tawdry.

What was he thinking about over there? The more he thought about it, the more she became convinced he was going to turn her down. It was time to activate the femme fatale sequence, and Houston better not have a problem this time.

"Nic," she said.

"Yeah?"

"It occurs to me that if you're undecided, you might want to get a taste of what you'd be giving up if you turned me down."

His green eyes clouded, and his nostrils flared. Those were good signs, right? She rounded her desk and stood behind him. Her fingers circled his waist and traveled up to his chest.

Then she pressed herself against him, reveling in the contact.

Encouraged by his sharp intake of breath, Gracie's fingers slid from the solid expanse of his chest to his taut stomach. Her fingers burrowed under his shirt and traced the defined muscles of his smooth abdomen. His muscles contracted as her fingers skated over them.

"Nic?"

"Yeah?"

His voice shook, and Gracie smiled. Definitely a good sign.

"How am I doing so far?" she asked.

"I'm impressed. But I'm not totally convinced yet."

Gracie trailed a finger down his stomach to the zipper of his jeans. His jeans were no match for the impressive erection that pressed against them.

She moved her hand up and down the contours of his erection, applying gentle pressure at the base of his cock. "Not impressed, huh?"

Nic leaned over and placed the palms of his hands on her desk. "Keep going," he whispered.

Gracie's head swam. She'd weakened him. Aroused him. And that knowledge spiraled through her body, awakening every erogenous zone, from the tips of her nipples to the bundle of nerves between her legs. She throbbed—everywhere. Every stretch of skin tingled as though she were made of nothing but pulse points.

Her hand worked him, kneading and rubbing his cock through his jeans. Nic's knees buckled and she dipped with him. Her fingers pulled on his zipper. "Enough," he said as he spun her to face her. "What else you got?"

Gracie bit her lower lip. What next? "A kiss?" she asked.

"Good idea. It could be a deal breaker. We'll see where we go from there."

She nodded and lifted her head toward his. "I'm a nibbler."

Nic gazed at her lips, and his pupils flared. "Nibble away. Don't let me stop you."

His height forced her to stand on her toes. For a woman who'd been taller than most of the boys in her class in high school, that particular physical trait provoked a flurry of sensual images to flash through her mind. Sex against a wall. It was a possibility. And given the breadth of his shoulders, she imagined he'd hold her up just fine. Oh, glorious day.

Pressing into him, she licked his lips, beginning in the center of his top lip and circling his entire mouth. He parted his lips, and Gracie took the opportunity to nip at them. His guttural moan rumbled through her, reminded her that she had so many places on his body still to explore. His soft lips brushed against her own, teasing and taunting her. Then she slipped her tongue inside his mouth, seeking to regain control.

Nic wrapped a hand around her ponytail and angled her face away from him, closing his mouth over the skin just below her ear. Gracie breathed and his hair tickled her nose. His scent—a natural musk with hints of orange—wrapped around her like a warm blanket. She snuggled into him, and his arms enveloped her.

A series of knocks on her office door yanked her out of the moment. They sprang apart and paced to opposite sides of her office. "Yes?" Gracie called out.

Brenda poked her head in. "Gracie, Ms. Rubio has a question about next week's schedule. Are you available?"

Gracie grabbed her ponytail and draped it over her shoulder and down her chest. "I am, Brenda. Be right there."

Nic stared at her, undermining her effort to get a handle on herself. His features revealed nothing, but his flushed face spoke volumes. He nodded his head, but she had no clue what he was assenting to.

"We begin this weekend," he said. "And get plenty of rest. You'll need it." He winked at her and strolled out the door, implanting a delightful image of his jean-clad ass in her brain.

Oh, my.

CHAPTER SEVEN

Ethan needed a sign. Something. Anything. An hour before his date with Gracie, he paced inside his walk-in closet, asking himself the same question over and over again: Should he go through with their arrangement?

He trailed his fingers over the row of tailored suits that made up his regular wardrobe. Bypassed the monogrammed shirts. Removed the Breitling watch he'd purchased with his very first bonus all those years ago. And as he rooted through his closet to find an old pair of jeans, he was keenly aware that his relationship with Gracie was based on a façade.

He froze. Relationship? What relationship? Gracie wanted a short-term arrangement. He did, too. They *both* wanted to explore their attraction and enjoy each other. What was so complicated about that?

If he thought for one minute the board would approve a sizable donation to Gracie's organization, he would have made up some excuse to renege on their agreement. But as far as the board was concerned, his stint at LTN needed to be over yesterday, and the board's chair had asked him not to draw attention to himself, probably because Ethan had suggested he had an easy way to accomplish that. So now he was Nicholas Hill. What a mess.

He wasn't any closer to resolving his dilemma when he got out of the shower. With a towel around his waist, he dried his hair and avoided his reflection in the foggy mirror.

The ring of his phone jerked him out of his thoughts. Hearing the tone he'd assigned to close family members, he immediately picked up. "Hello?"

"Hey, Ethan. Just checking in on my big brother."

His sister's cheerful voice always made him smile. "Since when, Em?"

"Scratch that. You're right. I'm way too busy to be checking up on the likes of you. Sophie begged me to call, but then she fell asleep. She wanted to talk to you, I swear, but by the time I got around to it, the kiddo had collapsed on the couch. Dear God, she had a traumatic night."

"What happened?"

Hearing the clank of dishes in the background, Ethan pictured his sister in the kitchen, phone pressed between her ear and her shoulder to hold it in place.

"I refused to give her Nutella for dinner and she lost it. Cried when I gave her spaghetti instead. Do you have any idea how disgusting it is to watch a child cry and eat spaghetti at the same time? Too many things dangling. Seriously, it was a consider-having-your-tubes-tied moment."

Ethan saw the scene play out in his head. Sophie did have a flair for the drama. "Never a dull moment in your household, Em."

"Ain't that the truth? So what's going on with you?"

"If you must know, I have a date, and I'm going to be late if I don't get off the phone soon."

"One of those high-society types skilled at making you act like a jackass?"

Em always considered herself his protector and moral compass, no matter that she was the younger of the two. "Hold back you're feelings, why don't you, Em?"

"Sorry. I'm usually not that judgmental."

"Bullshit."

She cackled. "You're right. Such bullshit. Okay, so if she isn't a prima donna, who is she?"

"Someone I met doing community service."

"Excuse me? Do you mean, actually serving the community? Or writing a check?"

"Ha, ha. Actually serving the community, wiseass. She's the director."

"Ooo. I like her already. There's a snag, though. I can sense it."

His sister always had a knack for ferreting out when he was troubled by something. "She has no clue who I really am."

"Meaning?"

Ethan lowered his head and gave a bitter laugh. "Meaning, she thinks I'm just a computer consultant who's done relatively well for himself."

Em whistled. "Yikes."

Her reaction didn't surprise him, and it only strengthened the ache in his gut. He'd regret this, for sure. "I get it, believe me."

"Well, look, you're obviously beating yourself up about this, so there's no need for me to pile it on. Be careful. If I know you, and I do, you're thinking about how this might hurt her later. But maybe this time around, think about how this might hurt *you* later, too, okay?"

"Thanks for the advice, Em."

"Always free and completely useless, big bro. I'll have Sophie call you next week."

"Give her a big hug and a kiss from her uncle, all right?"

"Will do."

He walked to his bedroom, mulling over his sister's observations. Em had a point. He'd been so concerned about hurting Gracie he hadn't considered how the charade might cause him pain, too. Just great. Now he had more to worry about.

He darted a glance at the alarm on his nightstand. Shit. No time to think about it now, though. With any luck, Gracie would reconsider her proposal and make the decision for him. But Ethan didn't bother to hold his breath.

* * *

The weekend had come too soon, and Gracie wasn't sure she'd ever be ready for her liaison with Nic to begin. Trying to avert a wardrobe crisis, she paced her apartment as she listened to Mimi on the line.

"Where are you going?" Mimi asked.

"He didn't tell me. He said casual would be fine. And he's picking me up in thirty minutes. Enough with the questions. Give me wardrobe advice."

"But how can I?" Mimi asked. "I don't even know where you're going."

"Mimi," Gracie said through gritted teeth. "I need help."

"Okay. What would you wear if you were meeting a friend for coffee?"

"Um. Dark jeans. And a silk blouse to dress it up."

"Then go with that. Make sure to show some cleavage, though. And heels. You need heels."

"Right. I've got to go."

Gracie ended the call and ran to her bedroom. She rummaged through her closet, praying her jeans were clean. Dark jeans? Check. Silk red blouse? Check. She sprinted to the bathroom and began removing her clothes. She looked down at her under-wear. *Uncheck.* The granny panties would have to go.

Slipping into the shower, Gracie tried to calm her nerves. Tak-ing deep breaths, she turned the shower knob just short of scald-ing. As the hot water ran down her body, she pictured the way the night would end. In Nic's bed. Or her bed. Or on the floor. It didn't matter. She pressed her hands against the tile and raised her face to the bathroom ceiling, soaking her hair in the steamy water. A shower. She'd love to shower with Nic. The slip and slide of their bodies. Argh. Thinking about Nic while she showered was not an effective way to calm her nerves.

As soon as the water cooled, Gracie jumped out of the shower, almost tripping on her bathroom rug as she reached for the towel. She dressed in seconds, knowing she would need plenty of time to dry her thick hair. Fifteen minutes later, she'd applied her lip-stick, given up on drying her hair completely, and walked across her living room floor so many times she wondered if her down-stairs neighbor would show up any minute.

Nic arrived at six o'clock. Exactly.

"Hi," she said as she opened the door.

"Hello."

"Come in. I just need to grab my purse and my jacket."

"Okay."

Nic's large frame filled the foyer. He wore a brown leather bomber and faded jeans. His cream V-neck sweater revealed a hint of the chest she'd explored yesterday.

"Where are we headed?" she asked.

Behind her back, she twisted her hands. They were clammy. *Grrr.* She smoothed her hands over her jeans as she listened to his answer.

"We have a dinner reservation at eight. I figure we could go bowling before then. It's a family favorite. I used to play a lot when I was a kid. Are you game?"

Gracie loved the idea, but she downplayed her excitement. Maybe this date wouldn't be as terrifying as she'd imagined. "Sounds like fun. You'll have to be patient with me, though. I haven't played in a long time."

He pushed off the wall and sidled up to her. "I was hoping you'd say that." Then he took her jacket from her hands and stood behind her. As she slipped her arms through the jacket's sleeves, he caged her in his arms. His warm breath drifted near her ear and she jumped. "Are you nervous?"

"What gave it away? The sweat on my upper lip?"

"Yes," he said.

She whipped around and stared him down.

He took a step back with his hands in the air. "I'm kidding." Then he grabbed the ends of the scarf she'd just draped around her neck and tugged her flush against him. "Why don't we get the kiss out of the way? From there, everything should go smoothly."

Oh, yes, please. She reached into his jacket and threaded her hands together at his waist. "I should say no just to spite you."

"Ah, Gracie, but you'd only be punishing yourself."

She couldn't help but to grin at his conceit. "Wow. Someone's cocky this evening."

"Hold that thought for a couple of hours. Trust me. It'll come in handy later."

She lifted her chin. "Are you stalling?"

He didn't answer. Instead, his mouth swept over hers as his hands rubbed her back. Gracie opened her mouth and welcomed him inside. His lips danced across hers like silk, and then he followed his careful ministrations with a gentle tug of her bottom lip. Gracie was startled by the attention Nic paid to her mouth. The kiss was not a means to an end. It was the end itself. And Gracie enjoyed every minute of it.

Pressed against him, Gracie knew Nic was as affected by the kiss as she was. She reached between them, seeking his hard length. Once again, though, he stopped her. "Bowling," he said in a rough voice. "We're going bowling. And we need sustenance. *Then* you'll see how cocky I can be."

Gracie laughed and pushed him away. He seemed to know exactly what to say to ease her jitters. "If you don't stop talking yourself up, I'm going to start to think you're all hype. Let's go."

* * *

After Gracie bowled her second strike of the night, Nic no longer made suggestions about her form. She maintained a straight face, enjoying his confused expressions when she bowled an impressive set. Served him right for assuming she wouldn't be able to keep up with him.

In between frames, they discovered they had a lot in common. "So is this what you usually do on the weekends?"

He made a big show of drying his hands. "I don't bowl that much anymore. But my dad taught me, and we try to play whenever I visit."

They'd both learned to love the sport from their dads. She considered that a plus, and it gave her insight into his childhood. "My dad taught me, too. He played in a league, and when I was old enough, he took me with him."

"He taught you well, it seems." He picked up his bowling ball, approached the foul line, and released it with a significant show of power behind it. The ball bounced into the gutter, and he dropped his head. When he turned toward her, he smiled.

As he walked toward her, Gracie held her breath and pretended not to be dazzled by the warmth in his gaze. This man had the capacity to devastate her if she wasn't careful.

He reached her and helped her stand. "Lest you think I suck at all sports, I should point out I'm an avid runner."

"That's great. I run, too."

He tipped his head back and stared at the ceiling, a playful grin telling her he didn't take himself too seriously. "Of course you do."

She considered suggesting they run together, but she held her tongue and prepared for her next frame. She couldn't assume that he'd want to, and more to the point, she had no business searching for ways for them to spend more time together. That wasn't part of their deal.

Thirty minutes later, Gracie stood outside the bowling alley as Nic tried to hail a taxi. The deal they'd struck weighed heavily in her thoughts. "That was fun," she told him. She jumped from foot to foot to counteract the cold—and to hide her nervousness.

"Speak for yourself," he grumbled.

"What's wrong?"

A taxi arrived at the curb, and Nic opened the door. Gracie rubbed her hands together and climbed in, grateful to get out of the cold. With his gaze fixed on her, Nic gave the driver the restaurant's address. When the taxi moved into traffic, Nic turned to her. "You played me."

Gracie placed a hand on her chest, pretending to be surprised by the accusation. "Played you? How?"

"You suggested you weren't very good. Then you whipped my butt."

"All I said was that I hadn't played in a long time. Plus, not being very good is relative. I'm not very good compared to my dad. How was I supposed to you know you're . . . uh . . . less than proficient . . . at bowling?"

Nic replaced his frown with a sly grin. "I get it. You only pretended to need my help so you could get close to my body. That's why you stuck your butt against me as I helped you with your form."

Gracie laughed. "Ha. Let's not be coy, Nic. You chose bowling because you assumed you'd get to rub against me. And you did. It just so happens that I followed all that fondling with a big ol' can of whoop-ass."

Nic threw his head back and laughed. A deep, guttural laugh

that made her toes curl. The streetlights flickered in the cab, casting spotlights on his features. Right now, the delicious column of his throat took center stage. Gracie leaned over and kissed him there. Nic stopped laughing. When she raised her head, she looked into his eyes. The more they stared at each other, the warmer the temperature in the cab seemed to get.

"I'm not hungry," she said. "We could skip the restaurant and order take-out later."

"Ah, Gracie. You've just made me a very happy man."

Nic leaned forward to speak to the driver. "Change of plans, my friend. We're headed to West End. Take Canal Road."

The driver peered through the rearview mirror. "You got it," he said.

Gracie slid down along the backseat and covered her face. Yep. She and Nic knew they were going to have sex, and now the driver knew, too. But she was less concerned about the driver's impression of her than she was about Nic's. She was not a vixen by any means. And she imagined Nic would pick up on that fact within seconds.

Maybe this was a mistake.

No, no, no. What would be the point of second-guessing herself now? She resolved to enjoy her time with Nic for what it was. Casual. Fun. Playful. He'd claimed he was cocky, right? Time to find out if he was telling the truth.

* * *

When they reached his building, Gracie had tied and untied her scarf more than a hundred times. After the change in dinner plans, they hadn't engaged in any more conversation in the taxi. Nic surveyed the city streets outside his window while she tied and untied her scarf. But she didn't miss the deep breaths he took, or the way he clenched and unclenched his fists as he gazed at the passing streets.

Even now, as Nic pulled her through the building's entrance, they didn't exchange a single word. She wasn't sure she would have been able to. Strung tight like a newly tuned violin, she worried she'd snap if he so much as breathed in her direction. Was that the reason for Nic's silence, too? She glanced at him and noticed what could only be described as raw determination in his stony face. And like any self-respecting woman who hadn't had sex for months, visions of fantastic orgasms danced in her head.

The clack of her heels against the polished marble floors prompted her to scan the lobby and take notice of her surroundings. Vintage chairs, and sofas with plush cushions, dotted one side of the space, grouped together to encourage conversation. Museum-quality artwork, reminiscent of the art she'd spent hours appreciating in New York, hung on the walls. And soft music floated in the air, its source undetectable to the human eye. She'd entered another universe. She slowed and tugged on Nic's hand. "You *live* here?"

He stopped and surveyed the lobby, the crease between his brows suggesting he was trying to see the space from her perspective. "I bought this condo from a friend, at a deeply discounted price, believe me. I wouldn't have purchased it otherwise. All this opulence makes me itchy."

"That's a very nice friend." She tugged him close and pressed her chest against his. "Man or woman?"

She was teasing him, but she couldn't help wondering if she'd overstepped her bounds. What did it matter whether the friend was a man or a woman? She had no right to ask. Then again, if he freaked out about it, she'd know not to ask these kinds of questions, teasing or not.

He didn't hesitate to respond. "Man, definitely. It's a bachelor pad through and through. When we get to my condo, you'll see what I mean."

"The guided tour can wait, don't you think?"

His eyes bored into hers. "God, I'm so glad you agree. If you'd wanted a tour first, I would have given you whiplash rushing you though the place."

She caressed his cheek, and he squeezed his eyes shut. It was a heady experience, witnessing his response to her touch. *Her touch affected him.* And the knowledge that it did aroused her in a way she hadn't expected. "Can we go upstairs now?"

In answer, he spun around and steered her in the direction of the bank of elevators ahead. The hint of recognition in the doorman's eyes disappeared when Nic raised his hand in his direction, cutting off whatever words the man was poised to say. "We're heading up, Sal. No time to talk." The doorman gave Nic a curt nod in response.

Nic stepped into the elevator, spun her to face the doors, and then drew her in front of him. When the doors closed, he pressed his lips against her ear. "I want you so fucking bad I can hardly walk."

A tingle skittered across her belly and her clitoris throbbed. She rested the back of her head against his chest. What was that sound? A whimper? From her? *Gah.* Her dignity withered on the floor. *Bye, bye, Dignity.*

She held her breath during most of the elevator ride. When it reached his floor, she worried she'd hyperventilate if they didn't act quickly. Gracie gulped in a breath when the doors opened, relishing the cool air that floated over her face.

Nic stepped around her and held out his hand. Her hand trembled as she took his. When the elevator doors closed, Nic pulled her to the side of the hall and backed her against the adjacent wall.

Nic's green eyes bore into hers. "I can't wait another second," he said. His mouth came down on hers in a rush. The butterflies in Gracie's stomach disappeared, replaced by a slow burn that traveled up and down the length of her body and ultimately settled in her throbbing clit. She didn't care if it burned, though. She only cared that he'd relieve her of this almost unbearable need to feel him all over her.

In that moment, Gracie's desire for him snapped her self-control. This man overwhelmed her senses, made her want to climb his body and burrow into him. And she wasn't going to waste this opportunity. But he was too far away, a problem she had the power to correct. Lacing her fingers, she drew them over his head and around his neck, closing the space between them. He growled at the contact.

She reveled in his lips as his hands slid to her waist. Then his hands lowered to her sex, and Gracie's legs failed her. His strong hands held her tighter, helping her stay upright. She began to undulate her hips against his hand, urging him to do more, and he complied without hesitation. He used his fingers to echo her movements, pressing them against her clit through the fabric of her pants. His fingers were strong, sure, working in tandem with the denim to produce the friction her body craved.

Gracie couldn't remember wanting anyone this badly. His forearms were damp with sweat, much like hers, a consequence of the body heat trapped between them. And she didn't care. In fact, she welcomed the possibility that their lovemaking would be wanton and messy. What mattered was the tingle between her legs. The bundle of nerves there pulsed, making it difficult for her to think beyond her need for release, beyond her desire for that most pleasurable sensation to wash over her. If he could produce this level of arousal in her through touch alone, would his cock send her over the edge? She guessed so, but suspecting was not enough. She wanted him inside her, and she prayed he wouldn't retreat again, because if he did, she'd clobber him.

* * *

Ethan moaned, goaded by the pressure of his dick against the zipper of his jeans. Gracie was so responsive she'd made him combustible. When he increased the pressure against her clit and began circling it, she whimpered. He'd unlocked the sweetest sound. Then her hands lowered to his crotch and stroked him, and for a second he threatened to whimper, too.

It wasn't enough, would never be enough, but they were in the hall outside his apartment, and this wasn't the place for what he had in mind. Still, he found it hard to stop touching her, greedy for every possible second of contact with her. He increased the rhythm of his fingers yet again, causing her to drop her head against his chest.

"Nic, it feels so good," she said against his ear.

The statement hit him in his gut—and reminded him that he'd misled her. She wanted to be in Nic's arms, the laidback computer consultant with a speeding problem. She didn't want Ethan, CEO of Media Best and man with a troubled past.

He backed up, needing to separate their bodies so he could think. Her small cry of protest echoed the turmoil in his brain. She reached for him and pulled his torso close to hers. She was fucking amazing. He wanted to spend days in bed with her, with her legs wrapped around his, as he studied her curves and learned what she liked.

As if sensing his thoughts, she looked up and regarded him with a knowing expression. "You're thinking too much, Nic. This is exactly what I want. Sex. That's all. Whatever's bouncing around in that head of yours, shut it down."

The heated gaze in her seductive eyes spun a web around him, ensnaring him. And like easy prey, he accepted his fate. He'd think about the consequences later. "Let me get you inside."

She slowly nodded her agreement as he patted his jeans in search of his keys. With one hand, he unlocked the door. With the other hand, he pulled Gracie inside.

He wanted a bed. They didn't make it past the foyer.

There, against the front door, he resumed his thorough exploration of her lips, swirling his tongue with hers and only coming up for air when she pulled his shirt over his head. Gracie didn't wait for him to reciprocate. She whipped her own blouse above her head and moved her fingers over the cups of her lace bra. Ethan swallowed. This was going to be so fucking good.

His hands skated over both breasts, and her brown nipples

puckered. Unable to resist, he rolled her nipples with his fingers and watched them tighten to stiff peaks.

"Yes, that feels so good," she said.

Gracie pressed her palms against the door for support. Worried that she'd slide to the floor, he wedged his thigh between her legs and offered her a makeshift seat. The pressure of her ass against his thigh aroused him. But her ass writhing on his thigh nearly undid him. A tremor ran through his body, a preview of the vibrations that would floor him when he buried his cock in her heat.

To Ethan's surprise, Gracie pushed him away.

"What's wrong?" he choked out.

"Nothing's wrong. I want a chance to explore you. Let's switch places."

All the blood in his body rushed to the massive erection he already sported. Without further prompting, he spun around and leaned against the door. Gracie bent her head and licked the contours of his chest.

She fell to her knees and placed her hands on his waist. Ethan imagined her plump lips sucking him off, but that wasn't going to happen. Not yet.

Ethan dug his fingers in her hair and watched her lick and suck his skin. He gave her a minute. He'd counted. Careful not to hurt her, he wrapped the ends of her hair around his fist and coaxed her to a standing position. "Sorry. If I'm going to have any chance of lasting, we're going to have to move on."

Gracie sighed. "If we must." She pouted, but her hands shook as she trailed them up his thighs and rose to her full height. If he hadn't been paying such close attention to her responses, he would have missed the slight exhale of breath, and the shakiness of her laughter. He abhorred the possibility that she was nervous around him, but asking her about it would only make things worse.

"Believe me, we must," he said.

Impatient to see all of her, he dropped to his knees, unzipped her jeans, and unfastened the top button. He kissed her stomach, licking her belly button as he drew her closer to him. His finger traced the smooth skin of her belly, and then he tugged her jeans down her thighs. She squeezed his shoulders, resting her hands against them for purchase as he helped her step out of her jeans. Like a gift he didn't deserve, she stood there in lace panties and high-heeled shoes. "I'm shredded," he said as he rose and studied her. "I could come from this image alone."

She gifted him with a sultry smile. "Or you could come inside me."

"Yeah. I think I'll take you up on that offer." He pulled her toward him, but she backed away, bumping her ass on the entry table. He moved toward her as he unbuttoned his jeans. "Get on the table," he said.

Gracie looked behind her. "Doesn't look comfortable."

"Or we could take sixty seconds to walk to my bedroom."

In answer, she stood on her toes and shimmied backward onto the table, stretching her arms out to him. He moved into her embrace and slipped his fingers through the waistband of her panties and tugged. She gasped as he ripped the panties from her body. "You know what's going to unglue me?" he asked.

"What?"

"The thought of you going anywhere without these," he said as he lifted her panties in front of him. Then he placed them in one of his back pockets and reached for a condom inside the other. As he did so, he searched her face, gauging whether she was as aroused as he was. She panted. She squirmed. Her teeth tugged on her bottom lip. And the scent of her arousal wafted through the air. No question, they were on the same page.

Ethan couldn't prolong this further. He lowered his jeans to his thighs, rolled the condom on, and lifted Gracie's legs as he centered his cock at her entrance.

Gracie nudged her ass closer to the table's edge, spread her legs farther, and pressed her hands on his shoulders, giving them a firm squeeze. Then he entered her, and her breath hitched. "Unreal," he whispered.

"Yes," she agreed.

"Ready for more?"

Her eyes grew wide. Then she slid her arms around his waist and grabbed his ass, helping him enter her to the hilt.

"Fuck, woman. You're impatient," he said as he began to thrust into her.

Her head came down on his shoulder. "Don't stop. Please."

"More? Harder?"

She nodded against his shoulder. "Yes, yes, please."

He increased the tempo of his stroke, gritting his teeth against the torturous sensation when the ridges of his cock pressed against her walls. Then he stopped. "Give me a second," he said.

Gracie's head lifted from his shoulders. "That's cruel," she said.

"It would be cruel if I came too fast. Okay. I'm good."

"Carry on, then," she said. The laughter in her voice touched him, made him want her even more—and he hadn't thought that would be possible.

He nipped her neck and began to stroke her in earnest. Their moans mingled in the air, punctuated by a slide of skin here and a sucking noise there. Her breasts bounced in front of him, and Ethan knew he wouldn't last much longer. He'd make up for this later. He covered her mouth with his, wanting them connected in as many ways as possible.

"Moan for me, baby," he said. "Let me know you're loving this just as much as I am. Breathe it into me." And she did what he asked of her. A low-pitched moan fell from her lips, and a tremor skated up Ethan's spine. "I am going to come so fucking hard, Gracie. So. Fucking. Hard."

"Nic," she panted.

No, not Nic. Ethan, dammit.

"Nic," she said. Her voice rose and fell, as though she were rolling his name on her tongue, savoring him, savoring this. He hated that name. But he wouldn't stop. *He couldn't stop.*

Her moans grew, rising above the other sounds in the hall—the intermittent bang of the table against the wall, the rustle of his jeans, and the clank of his belt, which still hung from the jeans scrunched at his thighs. "Oh, shit, Gracie. I'm going to come. C'mon, baby. I'm waiting."

Gracie banged her hand against the table. "Oh, yes, Nic. Yes, that's it." Then she began to shake, the muscles in her legs tightening around his waist. He couldn't bear it any longer and released a hoarse cry, letting the streak of lighting pulse through him. Then her orgasm chased his as she squeezed her eyes shut and screamed his name once more.

The pleasurable tingle in his body fled in that instant, and a frisson of dread skated up his spine in its stead. But he summoned the strength to shake it off. This relationship was due to expire in less than four months. Her rule. She wanted the comfort of a man in her bed, but she had no room for one in her life. Now that he thought about it, they were more alike than he'd first realized. So he'd give in to the pleasure they both craved, and then he'd move on. Guilt had no place in the equation.

He kissed her neck and breathed in her scent. The familiar stirring in his cock surprised him. So soon? No freaking way. "Hang on, I'm going to carry you to the bedroom."

She pushed against him. "Excuse me?"

He caressed her cheek. "I said I'm carrying you to the bedroom. My home, my rules."

Her glazed expression cleared. "I'll let that slide, but only because you just gave me one of the best orgasms of my life."

Her lighthearted comment gutted him, but he refused to show it. Of course she'd had other orgasms, he told himself. She'd never suggested she was a virgin, nor did he want her to be one. Still, imagining her with other men fucked with his head. His sister's warning immediately came to mind, reminding him that he had to protect himself, too.

He lifted her in his arms and pressed his chest against hers. "Let's see if I can clinch the title as best orgasm giver of them all. When I'm done, any man after me will pale in comparison."

And when her mouth soured in response, he pretended not to see it.

CHAPTER EIGHT

Gracie rested her hands on her chin and stared out her office window. Images of her weekend escapade with Nic bombarded her brain. What she wouldn't do for another round or two—or three, really. She wriggled in her chair, adjusting her body in a fruitless effort to dampen her arousal.

Over the course of the weekend, she'd discovered Nic possessed more than enough stamina for them both. And she'd learned the extent of her flexibility, contorting her body like she'd been auditioning for a stint with Cirque du Soleil.

There'd been one tense moment, when she'd been tempted to squeeze his balls for a comment about the men who would come after him, but otherwise she'd gotten exactly what she'd hoped for.

Now came the hard part. How would she manage to see him in the office and pretend they hadn't been screwing the light fantastic all weekend? Would the Gray Ladies suspect that she and Nic had moved beyond friendship? If Calliope sensed something between them, she'd pounce on Gracie and force her to confess.

The woman was relentless, and she had a nose that could sniff out all manner of intrigue.

Gracie knew she couldn't hide in her office forever. She would have to share the same space with him at some point. But she didn't relish that fact. Not when she craved his touch. Not when the images of their lovemaking seemed permanently embedded in her mind. He was here. That knowledge alone was enough to make her ache.

Brenda buzzed her phone, and Gracie hit the speaker button. "Yes, Brenda?"

"Gracie, there's a gentleman named Mark Lansing here to see Nic. Says he needs to speak to him about a work issue, but Nic's running a workshop." Brenda's voice lowered to a whisper. "This one's smokin', too, Gracie. Looks like an extra from *Magic Mike*." Brenda paused. "*XXL*."

Gracie laughed. Brenda's antics were a welcome distraction. "Be right out, Brenda."

Gracie walked to the reception area and stopped short when she caught her first glimpse of Mr. Lansing. This man *worked* with Nic? She slowed to gain some extra time to study him. He wore a navy business suit and checkered cufflinks that matched his red tie perfectly. But he stood in a relaxed pose, his jet-black hair flopping carelessly over one brow, a perfect complement to his devilish smile.

He played the part of the successful businessman well, but she suspected the suit masked an earthy, hot-blooded male who could make a woman pant just from his hooded gaze. What surprised her most was the briefcase at his side and the stack of papers in his hands. He was here to attend to business. With Nic.

She'd pictured Nic working at home—alone. But Mr. Lansing's presence made clear that wasn't always the case.

She stretched out her hand. "Mr. Lansing, my name is Graciela Ramirez, the director of Learn to Net."

Mr. Lansing shook her hand, but there was neither a tingle nor a spark between them. The zing, apparently, was reserved for Nic. "Call me Mark."

"And you can call me Gracie. Is this an emergency? Do I need to grab Nic from the computer room?"

"I wasn't sure how long he'd be here. I need to go over some paperwork with him. If you have an empty room, I could wait there. He won't be going past the lunch hour, right?"

"The workshop shouldn't take more than an hour, and he's been in there for forty minutes already." Gracie turned to Brenda. "Brenda, could you take Mark to our conference room?"

Brenda jumped out of her chair. "Of course," she said. "I'm an eager beaver." Under her breath, she told Gracie, "Pun intended."

Gracie snorted and turned back to Mark, who was watching their exchange with a wry grin. "Sorry, Mr. Lansing. It's been a strange day. There's a phone in the room. And if you need water or coffee, we'd be happy to get it."

Mark thanked her as Brenda waved him in front of her. "We're just going down this hall," Brenda told Mark. As they walked down the hall, Brenda, wide-eyed and flustered, turned around and pretended to swoon.

Gracie shook her head. Brenda was incorrigible.

Gracie decided to peek in on the workshop on cybersecurity. It had been Nic's idea. He'd heard countless stories of older people scammed out of savings because they'd revealed personal information online. Gracie had agreed with him that the workshop would be useful to LTN's clients, both young and old.

On the one hand, she embraced the cyberspace revolution, had fashioned her nonprofit career around it. On the other hand, she feared some of its implications, not the least of which was an impingement on an individual's right to privacy. Surely everything about a person shouldn't be discovered with just a few clicks of a mouse. Mimi chastised her for not researching potential dates. She countered that there was a time, not long ago, when people got to know others simply by spending time with them.

She tiptoed into the room and sat in the back. Nic acknowledged her with a nod and a warm smile. She waved hello in return and dipped her head.

Calliope raised her hand.

Nic's gaze whipped to the ceiling. "Yes, Calliope?"

"How much information should you provide when you create an online profile?"

"Good question," he said. "There are a few ways to protect yourself..."

Gracie watched Nic cross the room as he spoke. He engaged the class, pausing to make sure they were following his tips and stopping every so often to ask if anyone had questions. He owned the room, and she wondered whether he'd done anything like this before.

Returning her attention to the workshop, Gracie noted that a few of the participants even jotted notes.

"Go ahead and search for your name on the Internet. It's an interesting exercise to see what information is out there about you.

If it's more information than you'd like, there might be ways to correct it."

After a minute, Calliope chuckled. "Ha. Apparently, I'm a porn star living in Las Vegas."

Mr. Crandon's eyes widened. Then he leaned over to view Calliope's screen. Calliope pushed him away. "Oh, no, sweetie. You couldn't handle that. You've got more than enough right next to you."

Nic squeezed his temples with one hand while Gracie stifled the giggle that bubbled in her throat. When Ms. Rubio raised her hand, he rushed to her side. After a few seconds of discussion with her, he leaned over and tapped on her keyboard.

"Nic, what's your last name?" Calliope asked.

He responded without hesitation. "Hill."

"Let's see what I find when I look up Nicholas Hill," Calliope said. She began to type.

Nic rose to his full height, a deep frown marring his handsome face. "Actually, Calliope, we've got to wrap up the workshop. The computer room needs to be cleared out for the lunch crowd."

Calliope pouted and stood. "Spoilsport. Tell me this, Nic. Do you know how to have fun? Because I'm sensing a lot of tension bottled up inside of you. You might want to find a way to release it. Just a suggestion."

Calliope winked at Nic, looped her arm through Mr. Crandon's, and left the room.

As Gracie walked to him, Nic raised his head to the ceiling and muttered an unintelligible word.

"Calliope doesn't mean to annoy you," Gracie said. "She's just sassy."

Nic smiled, revealing the adorable dimples that highlighted his remarkable smile. "That's the understatement of the year." As the rest of the workshop participants shuffled out the door, Nic's gaze went from friendly to intimate. "It's hard not to touch you right now."

Heat snaked through Gracie's core. He wasn't playing fair. And to her surprise, she wanted to play, too. She leaned into him and whispered a suggestion. "My office is down the hall. You could touch me there. But just a touch."

"Let's go," he said as he sailed through the door.

Gah. She'd forgotten about Mr. Lansing. Mark. "Wait a minute. You have a visitor. Mark Lansing."

The color drained from Nic's face. "I do? Where is he? What did he say he wanted?"

"He's here on business. Brenda set him up in the conference room. He didn't say much."

The planes of Nic's face smoothed. "Okay. Thanks. I'll go check in with him. Shouldn't take long."

Gracie dismissed his sudden change in mood. "Looking forward to it."

* * *

Ethan's heart banged against his chest. Luckily, Mark hadn't blown his cover. Still, he didn't think he could stand much more of this ploy.

When Ethan entered the conference room, Mark raised his hand, signaling that he was on a call. Ethan sat across from him and stewed.

After Mark disconnected the call, Ethan leaned forward. "What's going on, Mark? Why are you here?"

Mark donned a look of earnestness. "Sorry to disrupt you on your service day. I know how much community service means to you."

"Cut the crap, Mark. What's going on?"

"I need your signature on the quarterly report. You approved the financials last week, but you wanted to see the final language in the summary. It has to be distributed to the board before tomorrow's meeting."

"Why didn't you send someone from the office? You didn't have to come here yourself."

Mark sat back in his seat. "Oh, really? Is there someone else in the office who knows that you're Nic Hill?"

Ethan swore under his breath. "I'm not cut out for this shit. I can't keep it straight in my head."

"So why don't you tell her?"

"And how do you propose I do that?

"Easy. My name is Ethan Hill, the CEO of Media Best. Nicholas is my given name, the name I stopped using years ago. Forgive me."

"If only it were that easy. Be serious. I need time to figure this out."

"Well, while you're out saving the world and answering Batman's calls, may I remind you that you have a company to run? I can cover some of your work, but some of the shit you do is above even my pay grade. There's a stack of work on your desk that you haven't addressed in weeks."

"I know. Today's my only day here. I plan to catch up the rest of the week. Then I'd like to dig into the Teleconnectiv software launch."

"Ethan, we have engineers working on the software. You don't need to do that."

"I *want* to do it, okay?"

Mark's lips pressed into a thin line. "Okay. Fine. Just read the summary and sign off, please."

Ethan read while Mark stewed. After several minutes, Ethan looked up. "It's fine." He wrote his signature on the executive cover page. "Anything else?"

"Nope," Mark said.

Ethan studied Mark's face and knew his friend was holding something back. "What's wrong? Something's obviously bothering you."

Mark stuffed the papers in his briefcase. "Look, I know you. And I know what you're like when you're dissatisfied. I was there. Remember? If you're unhappy about the job, do something about it."

"The job's fine. Just stressed, is all. I'll get over it."

"Fair enough. But if you need to get over anything, find productive ways to do it this time around."

"You're a fucking nag, man. I'll handle my own business, if you don't mind."

Mark's eyes closed. "Fine. See you at the office."

Ethan knew he was being a prick. Mark didn't deserve his ire. None of this was Mark's fault. Before Mark walked out of the conference room, Ethan called him back.

"What?" Mark asked through gritted teeth.

"Thanks, man. For everything."

Mark's mouth softened. "You got it. Catch you later."

Ethan rubbed his shoulder. Then he heard a knock on the conference room door. One of his favorite LTN students stood at the threshold.

"Hey, Jason. What's up?'

"You got a minute, Mr. H?"

"Sure. Come join me. Aren't you supposed to be in school today?"

Jason sat across from him, in the same seat Mark had been in moments ago. "It's parent-teacher conferences. I get a break."

"Ah. What's on your mind?"

Jason licked his lips. "I've been thinking about college a lot. About what I want to do. For a career, I mean. And I was wondering why you decided to work with computers."

Ethan had an easy answer. "I loved working with computers. It was as simple as that. I'll never forget my first computer class in high school. We learned how to make video games. I was hooked. The teacher taught the basics about game code, and then we moved to 2D and 3D graphics."

Jason nodded enthusiastically, appearing as eager as Ethan had been years ago. "Is that what you do now?"

Hardly. He signed documents, ran meetings, and answered questions all day. And if he was lucky, now and again he'd sit in on a meeting with his engineering staff. But that wasn't the point of his conversation with Jason. He wanted to encourage Jason to pursue his interests. "By the time I went to college, I knew I wanted to work in the computer industry. And when the Internet exploded, I learned as much as I could about designing software that would work on that platform. Now I concentrate on Internet communications, mostly instant messaging and video and voice calls."

"Cool. Any advice on how to make myself the ideal candidate for a spot at a top school like MIT?"

"Yeah. Work your ass off. Get good grades. Rock the SAT and your AP classes. Try to get an internship in the computer industry. And make sure your admission essay shows how much you love computer programming. Easy."

Jason rose and clasped Ethan's hand. "Right. Thanks, Mr. H. This has been helpful. I'm going to check out MIT's admission requirements while I'm here."

"Good idea. One more piece of advice."

"I'm listening," Jason said.

"Make sure you love what you do. If you don't, the job will wear on you. So long as you're inspired, you'll be golden. Even when things are harder than you'd like them to be."

"That's great advice, Mr. H. I'll keep that in mind."

Jason rushed out the door, a bundle of energy and inspiration. Ethan had felt like that once. Energized and inspired about his work.

He envied Jason's enthusiasm about his future. And frankly, that envy was a source of embarrassment. He was the CEO of a significant player in the Internet communications industry. Shouldn't he be satisfied with that? Why, then, did he miss the old days? The days when he sat around a conference room brainstorming with fellow engineers while eating cold pizza?

A soft knock on the door made him sit up. He turned and smiled. "Hey, Gracie."

"Can I speak to you for a minute?" she asked.

"Sure. What's up?"

"I'd prefer to speak with you in my office. If you have time, of course."

Her voice had lowered to a whisper. A very seductive whisper. Needing no more encouragement than that, he jumped up from his chair. "Of course. After you."

As he followed her down the hall, Ethan watched Gracie's hips swing like a pendulum. *The tease.*

"Nic, make sure you bring your papers with you," she said as she looked over her shoulder. "We can discuss them in my office."

Ethan cocked his head, wondering what the hell she was talking about. Then he saw Brenda at her desk. *Ah. Once again he was slow on the uptake.* "Right. I'll go get them from the conference room."

A minute later he closed her office door and leaned against it.

Gracie walked to him and pulled him away from the door. "I have a ton of work to do tonight, and Brenda's staying late to help. But you look like you need a kiss."

"You're so fucking smart it boggles the mind."

Gracie stepped into his waiting arms. Her upturned face calmed him. But her tight embrace stimulated him. Rather than begin something he couldn't finish, he pressed a soft kiss against her wet lips and rested his chin on the top of her head. The tension in his shoulders eased, and his breathing slowed. The moment was as perfect as any moment he could remember. Not the kind of sentiment a casual affair was supposed to inspire. But he couldn't deny the truth.

And the truth—that he could easily fall for Gracie—scared him. He stepped back, needing distance and a clear head.

Gracie's fingers absently rubbed her lips. "Enjoy the rest of the day, Nic."

"You, too, Gracie," he said.

In a rare moment of clarity, he knew what he had to do: make her come to him. He wouldn't call. He wouldn't suggest they get together. He'd claim to be busy. And when sufficient time had passed, she'd understand the depth of his determination to see her on the terms she'd laid out. Theirs was a casual affair. He wouldn't let either of them forget it.

CHAPTER NINE

The insistent banging at Gracie's door startled her. She sat up, flipped the blanket off her, and rose from the couch. A quick peek through the peephole settled her nerves. Nic paced in front of her door, waiting for her to let him in. She hadn't seen him in over a week, and she didn't want to see him today. Especially not today of all days.

Her sweatpants hung off her hips, and her knit top dwarfed her frame. She sniffled and hoped her voice would carry through the door. "Hi, Nic. I'm sick. Probably best if I don't let you in."

She stood motionless at the door and listened. The ensuing silence surprised her. Was he gone?

"Graciela, let me in," was his muffled response. "Please."

The urgency in his voice threw her, an easy feat in her already muddled state. "Okay. But if you get sick, don't blame it on me." She unlatched the lock and cracked the door open. "Are you sure you want to come in?"

Nic's strained face softened at the sight of her. "I'm sure."

She let him in and plopped on the couch, returning to her burrowed state under the thick comforter. "I'm too sick to be good company."

Nic towered over her as his gaze swept over her living room. "I don't need you to be good company. I wanted to check on you."

"How sweet. You were worried about me?"

He didn't answer. Instead, he bent over and pressed the back of his hand to her forehead. "Do you have a fever? How long have you been sick?"

She swatted his hand away. "Careful, Dr. Hill. There's this medical advance called a thermometer. I've used it, like a capable woman should. No need to get crazy, McDreamy. I don't have a fever. Just a good old-fashioned cold." She blew her nose to punctuate her point.

Nic smiled. "Aw. You're a grumpy sick person. It's adorable."

She gave him her best not-in-the-mood stare until he shifted in place. Satisfied she'd made him uncomfortable, she burrowed deeper into the comforter. He turned and surveyed her living room again.

Yes, it was a mess. No, she didn't care.

He moved around her living room, picking up plates and tissues and other items she hadn't bothered to put in their proper place. Every movement was accompanied by more force than necessary. He yanked tissues off the table and dropped dirty dishes into the sink. His abrupt movements grated her nerves. "What's your problem, Nic?"

"I haven't heard from you in over a week."

Hearing the bite in his words, Gracie closed her eyes. "Ditto. I've been sick. What's your excuse?"

Silence.

"Nic?"

He stuffed a paper plate in her trash and placed his hands on his jean-clad hips. Even sickness couldn't distort that pleasant image. He expelled a ragged breath, drawing her gaze from his hips to his face. "I was worried, okay? You didn't call. I waited. And when I realized you wouldn't call, I tried to reach you on your cell phone. It went straight to voice mail. I had no idea where you were."

Nic strode across the room and sat in the chair opposite her sofa.

Gracie hid her face in the folds of the comforter. "Why did you wait?"

"What?"

"You said you waited. Why did you wait? Why didn't you call me first?"

"I don't know. I thought we needed space. Figured you'd call me when you were ready."

"Correction. You figured I'd call when *you* were ready. And apparently that didn't happen, and now you're frustrated."

Nic threw his head back. "You're right."

"If you wanted time apart, all you had to do was ask for it. We're adults, Nic. I know you think you have to protect me from falling for you, but that's my job. Protecting myself, that is. Worry about yourself."

He rose from the chair and motioned for her to sit up. "Scoot down. Put your head on my lap."

She sneezed. "I have cooties."

"Woman, must you challenge everything?"

She sat up, and he slid on to the couch. Adjusting the pillow behind her, she settled into a comfortable position and dropped her head onto his lap.

He groaned. "Good Lord, your head weighs a ton."

She turned on her back and looked up at him. "Are you *trying* to get kicked out of here?"

His warm smile suggested he hadn't taken the question seriously. Before she could tease him further, he squeezed his eyes shut, as though he had a migraine.

"What is it?" she asked.

Several seconds passed before he gave her an answer. "When I didn't hear from you, I realized something."

"What?" she asked.

"I worry about you."

Based on the frown that accompanied his declaration, she assumed he wasn't happy about it. The knowledge that he didn't want to worry about her stung. But she wasn't a hypocrite, so she understood his reluctance to step outside the box they'd constructed for their relationship.

She turned on her side to face him and placed her hand on his stomach. "I worry about you, too."

He responded by threading his fingers through her hair, intermittently holding a few strands and watching them drop against her cheek.

"I'm sleepy," she said.

"Go to sleep. I'm not going anywhere."

Gracie reminded herself that he was talking about today, not forever. She shut her eyes, hoping sleep would help her forget that fact.

* * *

Gracie woke in her bed. True to his word, Nic slept beside her. She imagined him lifting her from the couch and carrying her to her bed as she continued to sleep. But her musings about such an intimate gesture didn't last. Did he carry her to the bedroom because he expected to have sex with her? Was that the plan all along? After all, what else would a single, healthy male want to do on a Saturday evening?

Gracie threw the comforter off her body and searched for her slippers. She dropped to her knees and groped the floor under her bed. "*Mierda. Donde estan mis chancletas?*"

She shimmied out from under the bed and met Nic's gaze. He lay across her bed with his torso perched over the edge of the mattress. "Care to translate?" he asked.

"My slippers. I can't find them."

Nic swung his legs over the edge of the mattress and stood. "I'll help you look for them."

Gracie savored the tempting image before her. His hair jutted in different directions, and a faint dusting of stubble covered his jaw. A blue and black flannel shirt and loose jeans completed the sleepy lumberjack effect. She returned her gaze to his eyes and straightened her stance.

"Feeling better?" he asked.

She swallowed. "Much better."

Gracie waited, wondering when he would make his move. But he didn't. Instead, he strode past her and bent over. When he stood, he held her slippers in his hands. She mumbled her thanks, and her stomach rumbled.

"You should eat," he said.

"I made soup yesterday. Want some?"

"I'd love some." He batted his eyelashes and tapped his stomach. "I'm a big fan of grilled cheese sandwiches, too."

"I'm not making you a sandwich, Nic."

He shook his head and turned her toward her bedroom door. Gracie's stomach somersaulted when his hands rubbed her shoulders. "Let's go, sick lady. I can make myself a sandwich."

Minutes later, they worked in companionable silence. She pointed to the pan, he rummaged through her fridge for cheese, and she handed him two slices of bread from her pantry. Watching him with her peripheral vision, she poured her soup in a bowl and placed it in the microwave. As soon as the microwave door clicked shut, she turned and watched him prepare his sandwich. He moved around her kitchen with ease.

The domestic scene freaked her out. She didn't want him in her kitchen. He'd leave memories there. But she couldn't kick him out. That would be rude, wouldn't it? Yes, of course it would.

With a spatula in his hand, he gave her a saucy smile. "The key to the perfect grilled cheese sandwich is—"

"Lots and lots of butter?"

He scoffed at her suggestion. "No. You have to know when to remove the sandwich from the pan. The cheese has to be gooey, and you can't burn the bread. It's a science."

"I had no idea making a grill cheese was so complicated. You make it look easy, though. Actually, now that I think about it, you look good in my kitchen."

Nic's hands stilled, and the spatula hovered over the pan. "This is the extent of my skill in the kitchen. But don't worry. One day you'll find a man who'll make you a three-course meal."

Gracie received the message: *That man won't be me, Gracie.* Okay, she understood what this was, but did he have to be so blunt about it? Saved by the beep of the microwave, Gracie grabbed a dishtowel and retrieved her bowl of soup. She set the piping hot chicken noodle soup on the counter and fished in the pantry for saltine crackers.

She avoided his eyes as she walked around the counter and sat on a stool. "There's water and juice in the fridge."

Nic removed the pitcher of water, set it on the counter, and sat on the stool next to her.

The air pressed on her from all sides. She sipped on the soup, but the broth lacked flavor. Her cold had compromised her taste buds. She wanted to throw the spoon in the sink and return to bed, but she didn't want Nic to know she was upset, largely because she didn't know *why* she was upset. A sideways glance revealed only a few bites of his sandwich remained. *It figured.*

Then it dawned on her. She was supposed to be having fun with him. She'd told him she wouldn't get attached. Promised there'd be no histrionics. And she'd meant it. How low would she be if she pulled a bait and switch now? That wouldn't be fair to him.

It was time to readjust her Spanx and keep their interactions light and airy. "When's your birthday?" she asked.

"November fifth. Why?"

"Just wondering."

"What about you?"

"May twelfth."

He said nothing. But he didn't have to. They both knew they wouldn't be celebrating her birthday together. By then, the affair would be over.

She wouldn't dwell on that fact. "Can you arrange to take the day off for your birthday? I'd like to take you somewhere."

He turned his face toward her. "I think I can swing it. Where would you like to take me?"

"It's a surprise," she said with a grin.

He returned her smile. "Keeping secrets from me?"

"Yep," she replied.

Nic's face flushed, and he lowered his gaze to his plate. "It's never good to keep secrets."

Gracie placed a hand over his. "What's wrong?"

She stared at his profile, catching the descent of his long eyelashes as he closed his eyes. Like a turtle withdrawing into his shell, he caved inward, shoulders slumped. Gracie ached to comfort him, but she didn't know what was wrong. She'd stumbled upon a private moment and wanted to retreat into the background, to let him wrestle his demons in his own way.

Nic straightened and lifted his plate. "I'm going to head out. Still have some work to do this weekend." He rose and placed his plate in the dishwasher. "I'm glad you're okay. I'll see you next week." He kissed her forehead and strode out of the kitchen. Seconds later, she flinched when the door clicked shut.

She wouldn't press him. It wasn't her place. She'd focus on having fun with him. Whatever issues he was grappling with, she was sure they had nothing to do with her.

CHAPTER TEN

Gracie hoped Nic would enjoy his birthday surprise.

"Where are we going?" he asked.

As she drove her car, she snuck a sideways glance to gauge his mood. He tapped his hands on his thighs as he peered through the passenger side window. Nic liked control, and in this moment he had none. Gracie liked having him at her mercy.

As she made her way onto the Beltway, Nic blurted out, "We're going to Virginia?"

"Yup."

"A vineyard?"

"Nope?"

"The Caverns?"

"Nuh-uh."

He sighed and tapped the dashboard. "Can you give me a hint?"

Gracie reined in the giggle that ached to escape her lips. "It's something you like to do."

"Something relating to computers?"

"C'mon, Nic. Where's your imagination? No more hints. Just sit back and relax. We'll be there in fifteen minutes."

Nic shifted in his seat, wiggling until he found the right spot. "Fine," he said. Then he peered out the window again. And he started tapping on his thighs again. This time, though, the nervous activity was accompanied by a cheerful whistle. After a minute, he caved. "A driving range?" he asked.

"No," Gracie said. "Give it up, Hill. We'll be there soon."

* * *

Gracie's car exited the Beltway. Ethan had no clue where they were headed. Gracie hummed as she drove, purposefully ignoring his repeated requests for more clues as to their destination. After a few minutes, the paved road met gravel. Then a sign came into view. THE BELTWAY INTERNATIONAL SPEEDWAY.

Ethan got out of the car and met Gracie at the driver's side door. "You're taking me to an auto race?"

"No. That would be boring." Her dark shades failed to hide the glee in her eyes. She held out her hand and smiled at him. What a compelling image she made. Her wavy hair danced in the wind, and her tan skin glowed with vitality. "Come with me," she said.

Ethan had no choice but to take her hand.

The racetrack was no more than two hundred yards away. He'd never been to one, and the silence surprised him. A tall, wiry man with a bushel of red hair and a warm smile greeted them at the entrance to the track. "Hiya, folks. You here for a track experience?"

Gracie stretched her hand out to the man. "We are. Well, he is.

My name is Graciela. And this is Nic. I've arranged for a half-day experience for him, in celebration of his thirty-second birthday."

"Well, all right," the man said. "My name's Tyler. What's your experience, Nic? Ever ride on a professional racetrack?"

Ethan stared at Gracie. She'd put a lot of thought into this, and he didn't deserve it. "I . . . uh. No, no experience on a track. I've always wanted to get on one, though."

"Ah, I've got a newbie," Tyler said. "That's always fun. Can you operate a manual transmission?"

"I can," he answered.

"Great. Your package includes an orientation that will cover the equipment and driver safety. You'll get fitted for a helmet and tracksuit. Then you'll have five turns out on the beginner course. How's that sound?"

Ethan searched for the right words but couldn't find them. "I'm. . . uh . . . I'm floored."

Tyler drew a baseball cap from his back pocket and placed it on his head. "She arranged a great surprise for you, didn't she?"

Ethan threaded his fingers through Gracie's as he pulled her to his chest. "Yes, she arranged the perfect surprise." Then he lowered his face and brushed his lips against hers.

"Well, all right," Tyler said with a smile. "Come on with me, then."

Tyler ambled ahead of them to a building to their right.

Ethan placed his arm over Gracie's shoulder. "This is too much, Gracie. My birthday isn't special. A gift like this must have been pricey."

Gracie smiled up at him. "Accept it and enjoy it. I insist."

He nodded, but his stomach churned. He didn't want her to

spend money on him. He didn't know about her financial means, but given that she ran a nonprofit, this gift was probably a setback. If he made a big deal about it now, though, he'd hurt her feelings, so he promised himself to address it afterward.

Forty-five minutes later, Ethan ambled toward the racetrack in a red and blue tracksuit. The suit was snug, but he didn't give a rat's ass about the fit. He was pumped. Adrenaline coursed through his veins. His inner roar matched the rev of the race car's engine. She was a pretty, sleek machine, and Ethan couldn't wait to get his hands on her steering wheel.

Gracie pecked his cheek. "Have fun."

Ethan watched her walk to the stands and sit on a steel bench. He turned and Tyler handed him a helmet. Crew members poked and prodded the racing car as another member tugged on Ethan's helmet to be sure it fit properly.

After a thumbs-up from Tyler, Ethan climbed into the car. The car's vibrations reverberated through his body, causing his heart rate to spike. He welcomed the whiff of engine oil that filled his nostrils.

One of the members gave Tyler the sign of a checkmark, indicating that the car was ready to go.

Tyler leaned against the car and pointed to the track. "The car is wired to maintain a speed no higher than a hundred miles an hour. You'll hear a beep if your speed approaches a hundred, then if you go over that, we'll flag you down. Fast and steady is fine. Too fast means you won't be able to control the car, and we can't have that. I'll coach you through it on the two-way."

Ethan adjusted his body in the car's cramped quarters. "Got it."

"Any questions?" Tyler asked.

"No. I think I can handle a hundred."

"*Under* one hundred is the goal."

Ethan squinted as he looked at the track. "I hear ya."

"Get your bearings and you should be all set."

His bearings. Right. He searched for Gracie in the empty stands. She tapped at her phone. Eventually, she looked up and waved. No one had ever given him such a thoughtful gift. That thought blew his mind. Poised to circle the track at a hundred miles per hour, he reined in the range of unfamiliar emotions barreling through him. Ethan checked his mirrors, located the clutch, and pushed the gear shift into neutral. And then he was off.

* * *

Ethan's gaze followed Gracie's backside as she climbed the stairs to her apartment.

She spoke over her shoulder. "Your birthday celebration isn't over."

"It isn't?"

"No, I have something else planned."

He tugged the bottom of her coat. "You've done enough."

She reached the top of the landing and spun around. "Don't stress. It's just cake."

Ethan smiled. "Did you make it?"

She slipped the key in the lock and pushed her front door open. "I'm not a baker. Cooking's my thing."

He followed her into her apartment and closed the door, shucking his jacket off and tossing it on the couch.

"I'll be right back," she said.

Ethan waited. It was the middle of the day on a Tuesday, and he hadn't checked his e-mail or voice mail. Not once. Incredible.

He circled her living room, taking in the homey space. He hadn't paid attention to the décor until now. But now he searched the space for clues about Gracie's personality. A red couch dominated the space, accented by brown and rust-colored fabrics. Gracie loved pillows. Like her office, the space included fun touches, including candleholders in the shape of people doing yoga poses.

Gracie padded into the room, and Ethan turned.

Fuck.

She stood barefoot, wearing a black negligee and a tremulous smile. "Hi."

Ethan swallowed. And swallowed. And swallowed some more. "Hi."

With her hands behind her back, Gracie took slow steps until she stood in front of him. "I'd like you to indulge me. Do you think you could?"

"Whatever you need, I'll make it happen. I promise."

Gracie licked her lips and her gaze darted around the room. With one hand still behind her back, she led him to the couch. "Come sit."

Ethan sat on the couch and waited. Gracie dropped her arms to her sides, one hand holding a black scarf. "I'd like to blindfold you."

"And do what?"

"That's just it. I don't want you to see what I'm doing. And I don't want you to expect it. I think it might be fun."

"Have you ever done anything like this before?"

"No. But I'd like to try it. With you."

A myriad of emotions battled in Ethan's head. *Don't do this, you selfish son of a bitch. She's telling you it's special for her. Let her give that to someone who's not lying to her. But she wants this. And how can you say no to her? She knew going into this that you wouldn't commit to her. She told you she didn't have time for more, didn't she?*

Her voice silenced the angel and the devil chattering on his shoulders. "Never mind. It was a bad idea."

"No, it's not a bad idea. It's a great idea actually."

Her tight expression transformed into a hopeful one, her big, expressive eyes confirming that he'd made the right choice. "Are you sure?" she asked. "Because we don't have to—"

"Gracie, I want to."

She bit her lip and nodded. "Okay." She held out the scarf. "Could you remove your clothes and put this on?"

Ethan watched the rise and fall of her chest. "Sure."

He removed his jeans. Next, he pulled off his sweater and T-shirt in one fluid motion. He folded the scarf several times, and then tied it around his eyes.

Gracie's warmth pressed against him. "I'm waving my hands. Can you see anything?"

"Not a thing."

"Good."

She held his hands and he dropped back onto the couch when the edge brushed against the backs of his knees.

Gracie padded away from him. She rustled in the kitchen. A utensil scraped against a plate. Sink water flowed. She banged a drawer shut. What the hell was she doing in there? A loud clatter followed several seconds of silence, suggesting she'd dropped something.

"Everything all right?" he asked.

She muttered, and then she said she was fine.

Her footsteps drew near and he tensed, unsure what to expect.

"I bought cupcakes," she said.

Ethan laughed. "Yeah?"

"Several kinds. I wasn't sure which you would like. I figured I could help you taste-test them."

"I'm ready."

"Okay. Here's the first. Open up."

Ethan opened his mouth and moaned when the rich chocolate cake touched his tongue. "Oh, that's good. The icing isn't chocolate, though. Buttercream, right?"

"How'd you know?"

"That's my favorite cupcake combination."

"Darn. I thought we'd be playing this out longer."

"No, no. Keep going."

"Okay. Here's the second."

This time, too, the aroma of cocoa clued him in on the flavor. But this was different. Slightly bitter with a sour cream frosting. "Red velvet?"

"Damn. You're good at this. We can stop now."

"Put some of the cream cheese frosting on your finger."

"And do what?"

"Put it in my mouth."

Silence.

"Gracie? Isn't this what you wanted?"

"Yeah. I'm just not doing a very good job of it."

"Yes, you are. There's nothing you have to achieve here. Just do what feels right to you. Whatever it is, I'll like it."

Ethan opened his mouth and waited. One of Gracie's slim digits moved in his mouth and he closed in on it, sucking the frosting off her finger as it retreated.

Then she painted his lips with frosting and pressed her lips against his. "Oh, that *is* good."

"Anything else you'd like to do?"

She didn't answer, but her legs brushed his knees, and the scent of lilacs permeated the air. *What was she planning?* She placed her hands on his knees, her hair feathering the tops of his thighs. His shaft stiffened and rose to the occasion. *Holy shit.* It was official: This was the best birthday ever.

Ethan's heart hammered in his chest. He wiggled his fingers, wanting to touch her, wanting to wrap her hair around his hands and tug her mouth to his cock. But he wouldn't. She controlled this moment. And damned if he didn't like the power she held over him.

Her hands, silky as always, spread his legs apart. She filled the empty space with her body. He wanted to see her on her knees, knew he would enjoy the picture she made. Without his sense of sight, his mind filled in the blanks, and the image he conjured made his cock hard.

"Nic?"

"Yeah?"

"I'm pulling down the straps of my negligee."

He swallowed. The image in his head transformed into a masterpiece. "Can I touch?"

She mumbled an unintelligible response.

"What was that?" he asked.

"I said yes."

Her voice glided over him, coaxed him to lean forward and reach out to her. Her breasts, round and heavy, filled his hands. His fingers circled over them, beginning with her nipples and moving outward. Her torso pressed against his knees, suggesting she was trying to move closer to his touch.

"Can I lick?" he asked.

"No."

Ethan lifted his hands. Had she changed her mind? Maybe she wasn't satisfied with the way the events had unfolded. He opened his mouth. Before he could ask her whether something was wrong, she pressed two fingers against his lips. His stomach muscles contracted when those two fingers trailed down his chin and slid to his chest.

Her soft whisper caressed his cock like a lullaby. "Tell me how you like it. Tell me how to please you."

Ethan began to speak, but the words lodged in his throat. He cleared it and tried again. "Hold the base of my cock. Squeeze it. But not too hard."

Her smooth hand wrapped around his erection. "Like this?"

An electric shock zinged through his body, firing every synapse. *Fuck, yes.* "That's perfect. Now move your hand up and down."

Gracie did as he asked. She applied just the right pressure. Her hand, delicate and soft, moved at just the right speed. Ethan fisted his hands and moaned. He couldn't help it. Something about not seeing her compelled him to make his pleasure clear to her. "Ah, Gracie. That feels good."

Her hand left his shaft and a whoosh of air passed across his chest.

"Are you leaving me?" he asked.

"No. I'm getting a pillow."

Her arms brushed his legs, and her hand slid up and down his cock again. Ethan wanted to bury himself in her wet heat. Wanted to slide in to the hilt and fuck her senseless. But he held himself in check, waiting to see where she would go. He didn't wait long. Her plump lips wrapped around the crown of his cock and sucked. Then she slid her tongue up and down his cock as she fondled his balls.

Ethan didn't see stars. He saw the entire solar system. "Fuck, fuck, fuck. It's yours, baby. Take it all."

And she did.

She took every inch of him, sliding and sucking as she moved from the base of his cock to the head. And she did it over and over again. Her hair brushed his stomach, and she raked her nails against his thighs. Ethan bent over and fisted her hair, rubbed her shoulders, reached for her breasts. *He needed to do something.* Something that would relieve the almost painful pressure that surrounded his cock. But he couldn't see. And she wanted him this way.

Maybe if he begged, she'd take pity on him. "Graciela. Please."

She pressed a kiss to his cock. "What do you need?"

"I need you to ride me. Right now."

The rip of the condom packet made him woozy. *Please, Gracie, hurry.* Then her thighs landed outside his, and his cock strained to find her heat. Her hands pressed against his shoulders, and she nestled her face in the crook of his neck. He breathed in the flowery scent of her hair and prayed she'd ride him hard.

He placed his hands around her waist and nudged her. "You're torturing me, sweetheart. I need you."

"You've got me," she said.

Then she sank down. Hard. Ethan's body warmed from his cock outward. Her slick walls teased and taunted. She pulled him in and held on tight, moaning her pleasure as he hummed his own. Every muscle in his body flexed in response to her movements. He grunted and groaned. Didn't give a fuck what he looked like, either.

"Too tight," she breathed into his ear.

He loosened his hold on her waist. "Kiss me, Gracie."

She leaned into him and placed her hands on the sides of his face. She explored his mouth, revered it, and when she came up for air, he panted. The pace of her breathing changed, grew shallow, needy, mirroring his own short breaths. He wasn't the only one strung tight.

"Gracie, I need you to fuck me. I need you to make me come, baby."

"I need it, too."

He searched for her clit. The minute he found it, Gracie cried out. "You're burning, aren't you, Gracie?"

"Oh, God. Yes, yes, yes. Please keep doing that."

His fingers circled her clit as she rode his cock. He pressed his face against her chest, licked his way to one nipple, then the other. She whimpered. And the sound made him want to beat his fists against his chest in triumph. Surely, she would kill him. The strain he was putting on every part of his body couldn't be healthy. He'd never recover. But fuck if he would tell her to stop.

She placed her hands on his shoulders, and her nails scraped his skin. He welcomed the discomfort. Anything to take his mind off the torture of being on the edge for minutes more than any man should bear. She adjusted her legs and rode him fast. Ethan wanted to cry in relief. Instead, he chanted his approval. "Yes, baby. That's it. That's it."

On the verge of the orgasm to end all orgasms, he drove upward, seeking the right angle to bring them both to release. At this rate, he would come before her. And he wanted them to reach that summit together. He found her clit again and rubbed.

"Oh, Nic. I'm going to come."

He wished he could block out the sound of her voice. Each time she shouted Nic's name, Ethan jerked as though she'd delivered a physical blow. He didn't deserve her pleasure, but he took it just the same.

"Hang on, Gracie. Not yet." He ripped off the scarf, needing to see her eyes when she came.

She drew back. Her slack mouth and glazed eyes betrayed her confusion. "What is it?"

"I don't want it to end. Let's slow it down." She pulsed around him and he gritted his teeth. "Ride me slow, baby."

She leaned forward, pressing her breasts into his chest. He wrapped his arms around her and kissed her fiercely. When they separated, she gulped in air and he rested his head on her shoulder. They remained still for several seconds, neither making a sound.

Before he could ask whether something was wrong, Gracie ground her hips and lifted herself off him, using his shoulders for support. "Is this how you want it? Slow?"

When she sank down, he choked out a curt "yes."

She continued to torture him several minutes more, whispering soft words of encouragement. Ethan couldn't hold off anymore. His body vibrated and his erection pulsed. Gracie's moans grew louder. She pressed deeper into his chest and angled her body, enabling her clit to rub against his pelvis each time she sank onto him.

To his surprise, she shouted her release before him. At its pinnacle, her orgasm seemed to move through him, forcing its way out of her and sweeping over him in the aftermath. He bucked against her, grasping her waist and lifting her up and down his length, unable to decipher when her orgasm had ended and his had begun. A storm of sensation rocketed through him, bringing him pleasure beyond anything he'd ever experienced. He wasn't sure he'd recover from this, from her.

Later that night, after moving to her bedroom, they spooned in her bed, spent and lost in their own thoughts. Abruptly, she turned toward him. "What were you thinking about out there, when you were driving the course?"

Ethan opened his eyes. He suspected she wouldn't believe him, but he told her the truth anyway. "Nothing."

"Nothing?"

"Absolutely nothing."

"Is that why you like to speed? Because it gives you a place where your mind shuts down?"

He'd never thought about it in those terms. In a speeding car, his mind focused on remaining on the road, hugging the curves, and avoiding a crash. And he relished the time to get away from the shit that burdened him. Behind the wheel, he escaped his job and the infinite responsibilities that came with it. "You might be on to something. It's therapeutic."

"Art is my therapy."

"How so?"

"Growing up, whenever I had a problem, I'd find my way to a museum. I went to high school in Manhattan, so after school, I'd go to the Met, or to the Guggenheim. And I'd walk, and walk, and walk. Study paintings, even the ones that didn't attract as much attention. There was something about seeing so much beauty, knowing it had been cultivated over years, an artist's passion captured in a painting or sculpture. It calmed me. Not sure why."

"Yeah, maybe that's what driving does for me. Sometimes my job can get overwhelming. And I don't love it as much as I used to."

"Could you do something else?"

Ethan couldn't imagine doing anything else. "It's not that easy, Graciela. I have a lot of people who depend on me. And what kind of person would I be if I hightailed it every time the job gets tough? My parents certainly didn't have that option. And they did shift work in a canned foods factory."

"So speeding is your escape?" she asked.

"Yeah, I guess. I take my frustration out on the road, which isn't wise, I know, but maybe that's why I do it."

He wanted to say more. To tell her that he hadn't felt the need to speed since they'd started spending time together. She balanced him. Made him yearn for a quiet life—with her in it. But sharing these feelings wasn't part of the bargain they'd reached, so he stuffed his soppy feelings away. "Thanks for making my birthday so special. I wouldn't have wanted to spend it with anyone else."

She blushed and dropped her face into the crook of her arm. "That's a nice thing to say."

Ethan nuzzled her ear. "It's true."

He stiffened when he realized the implication of his words. Each minute in Gracie's presence made it more difficult to envision the inevitable end of their affair. He didn't want to spend time with anyone else. She'd become his sanctuary. The place where he could be himself. The place where he could pretend there weren't duties and responsibilities tugging him in too many directions.

But Gracie didn't want more. And given that he was keeping a significant part of himself hidden from her, he didn't deserve more, either.

Gracie snuggled into him. "It's okay, Nic. I took it as a compliment, not as a profession of your love and undying commitment."

"That's not what you want, right?"

She hesitated. "Right."

"Same here."

Her eyes closed and a lazy smile spread across her face. He'd do anything to keep that satisfied look on her face. The thought of disappointing her weighed heavily on his chest. All he had to do was stick to the plan. Enjoy her now and leave her with pleasant memories of their time together. He prayed he wouldn't screw up.

CHAPTER ELEVEN

The next morning, Gracie's muscles ached. Everywhere. As she stretched, her core pulsed, still tender from Nic's relentless attention. She'd grin and bear that particular soreness.

Nic's side of the bed was empty, but the aroma of coffee filled her nostrils.

She sat up and readjusted the straps of her negligee, disappointed that she and Nic didn't have time to talk more. He'd opened up to her last night, had shared his fears about the growing chasm between him and his family. They didn't understand why he couldn't visit more. He didn't think they understood the pressure he was under. She'd suggested a surprise visit, when his schedule would allow, so it wouldn't be inconvenient for him, and so they wouldn't be disappointed if he had to cancel at the last minute. He'd told her he thought it was a good idea. And then his eyes had darkened, and there'd been no more talking after that.

Gracie wished they could stay in bed all day, but she had an appointment to prepare for. She reached for her iPhone on the nightstand. The screen indicated that she'd missed a call. Several calls. From Brenda. Gracie's heart pounded in her chest as she read the time: 9:42 a.m. She was late. *Shit, shit, shit.*

Gracie sprang from the bed and whipped open her closet door, grabbing the first pair of pants she could find. She didn't have to hear the message to know that Brenda was calling because she'd missed an appointment with the president of the Bentley Foundation.

With one leg in her slacks, Gracie called Brenda. Her assistant picked up after the first ring.

"Brenda. It's Gracie. I know I'm late."

"Gracie, is everything okay? I was so worried."

"I'm fine. I . . . I overslept. I set the alarm, but it didn't go off. Did Ms. Cantrell call?"

"Yes. She was looking for you. She said you'd have to reschedule the appointment."

Gracie dropped to the bed with a groan. "Did she seem angry?"

Brenda didn't say anything.

"Brenda, you there?"

"Yeah, I'm here. No, she didn't seem angry. Just a bit annoyed. Impatient. This is not like you, Gracie. What's going on?"

"Nothing's going on, Brenda. I overslept. Can you give me Ms. Cantrell's number?"

"Sure."

Gracie grabbed a pen and wrote the number down on the back of a receipt she'd found on her nightstand. "Okay, I'll call right now. Wish me luck."

"Good luck," Brenda said. Her voice, however, lacked any of the enthusiasm Gracie had come to associate with her assistant.

Gracie lifted her sluggish butt off the bed and finished putting on her slacks. What a nightmare. There was no time for moping, though. She needed to fix this. Steeling herself for an unpleasant call and expecting to reach Belinda Cantrell's assistant, she was surprised when Ms. Cantrell herself picked up the line.

"Ms. Ramirez, I missed you this morning." The woman's brisk tone highlighted the fact that she was not amused.

"Ms. Cantrell, I'm so sorry. I apologize. I overslept, and there's no excuse for it. All I can ask is that you give me a chance. For the sake of LTN."

"Ms. Ramirez, the Bentley Foundation gets thousands of requests each year from organizations seeking its support. A select number of them are invited to make proposals. An even fewer number of those inquiries result in an interview. You missed yours. I'm not inclined to give you a second chance."

Gracie's eyes watered. This couldn't be happening. This was her shot to save LTN, and she'd wasted it—because she'd spent the evening with a man who admitted he wanted nothing more from her than a casual affair.

The man in question chose that moment to walk into her bedroom with two steaming cups of coffee in his hands. She turned away from him and walked to the floor-to-ceiling window she'd always treasured. Today, however, she didn't appreciate the light that filtered through it. The sun was too bright, like a beacon shining down on her and her unfortunate lapse in judgment.

After taking a deep breath, she groveled. "Ms. Cantrell, I recognize that it was unprofessional of me to miss the appointment, but I can assure you nothing like this will ever happen again. I made a mistake. And I own up to it. I just need a second chance. I'll make myself available whenever you need me."

The ensuing pause made Gracie's stomach turn.

After what seemed like an eternity, Ms. Cantrell sighed. "Very well, Ms. Ramirez. I'll have my assistant call yours and propose another date. Don't miss it." And then Ms. Cantrell hung up.

Gracie released the breath she'd been holding. All was not lost. And things certainly could have been worse. Ms. Cantrell could have refused to meet her altogether. She'd been given a second chance, and she wouldn't screw it up.

With a roll of her tense shoulders, she faced Nic.

Wearing yesterday's jeans and T-shirt, Nic greeted her with a sexy grin. His mussed hair jutted in dozens of different directions, a visual reminder of the many times she'd run her fingers through it last night.

"Good morning, Gracie."

His voice slid over her like a protective veil. It comforted her. Made her forget her troubles. The difficult tasks she had to accomplish. And that was a big problem, because he wouldn't be around in six months' time, when LTN would border on collapse. He was too much. *They* were too much. Somehow their no-strings affair had transformed into a connection that tethered her to him, that made her want more.

She needed distance, both physical and emotional.

She reached for the second coffee mug in his hands. "Good morning, and thank you. Glad to see you're comfortable in my kitchen."

He nodded and sipped his coffee, watching her over the rim of his mug. "You had an appointment this morning?"

"I *missed* an important appointment this morning. I thought I set the alarm on my phone. Planned to be up at the crack of dawn to be sure I had more than enough time to go over my notes and get there early. The alarm on my phone didn't go off." She blew on the coffee, desperate to finish it quickly and head to the office.

His face turned ashen. "It was my fault. Your alarm, I mean. It went off, but I turned it off."

Gracie's mouth gaped. "You turned off my alarm?"

He set his mug on the side table and inched toward her. "I'm so sorry. I wasn't thinking. You looked so peaceful. I watched you for a bit, planned to wake you up with a kiss, but then I fell back asleep."

She slid backward, careful not to let the steaming coffee slosh onto her skin. He stopped advancing and planted his feet in the middle of the room.

Well, that was something, at least. She hadn't been a complete idiot. Still, what was she thinking having him over the day before a big meeting? And that was the point, wasn't it? She *hadn't* been thinking. "It's my fault, really. I should have timed your surprise better. Trying to do and be too much all at once. It's a continuing problem."

Gone. She needed him gone.

His eyes searched hers. "Is everything going to be okay? With the appointment?"

Gracie gulped the coffee and placed the mug on her nightstand. "It'll be fine." But that was just wishful thinking on her part. She strode to the closet and pulled out an outfit for work. "So I'm going to be busy this week. You?"

He stared into his mug. "Yeah. I'll be busy, too. Probably won't be able to come in for service hours. Is that okay?"

She didn't hesitate. "That's fine."

Nic cocked his head to the side. After several seconds of silence, he left her bedroom. By the time he returned, he'd donned his sweater and she'd dressed.

Nic's gaze followed her as she moved about the room. Ankles crossed, he leaned against her bedroom door in a lazy pose that was at odds with the chiseled angles of his face and the ever-present furrowed brow.

"Gracie?"

"Yes?"

"I'm sorry you missed your appointment."

"So am I," she said as she strode past him to the bathroom.

Minutes later, as she gathered her purse and coat, a million thoughts swirled through her head. They'd agreed to a casual affair, but it walked and talked like something else—something like a committed relationship. She'd easily slipped into the role of the girlfriend despite her claim of wanting nothing more than someone to warm her bed. And she'd wrapped herself in the cocoon of their temporary relationship, forgetting those aspects of her life that made her who she was.

She'd never missed a work appointment. And given LTN's dire situation, the mistake took on talismanic significance. If she didn't focus on LTN, she'd be doing exactly what Hector Ramirez assumed she would—letting her passion for a man overrule her common sense. When would she learn to focus on only one aspect of her life? It had to be work or her love life, not both. Never both.

She needed to get out of here, but first she had to face the man who stood at her apartment door.

She walked to him, unsure what to say. "So," she said.

"So," he replied.

Gracie sighed. "So I guess I'll see you when I see you." She winced when the words left her mouth. What an idiotic thing to say.

His eyes flashed in irritation, but he quickly regained his composure. "Right."

Before she could apologize, he lifted her chin and dipped his head. The kiss was unexpectedly tender. She didn't need it. But she wanted it. The purse at her shoulder dropped to the floor. She stepped into his space and threaded her fingers through the hair at the nape of his neck. Her eyes begged to close, but she forced them to remain open. Then she stepped back. "I have to go."

"I know you do," he said.

His voice, low and slow, held a hint of resignation. Good for him. At least one of them knew what was going on. As for her, she didn't know her ass from her elbow.

* * *

Any doubts about Nic's view of their relationship were extinguished later that week. After lunch on Friday, Brenda rang her office line. "Gracie, you have a special delivery."

For a minute, she wondered whether Nic had sent her flowers. He'd never done it before, but maybe he wanted to thank her for his birthday gift, which, she could tell, he'd thoroughly enjoyed.

She jumped from her chair and left her office. Brenda stood just outside her door with an ivory envelope in one hand. "Expecting something?" Brenda asked.

Gracie grinned. "No, Ms. Nosy. I'm not."

Brenda circled her and repeatedly sniffed the air. "I smell intrigue. I need gossip, Ms. Ramirez."

In response, Gracie shuffled into her office and softly closed the door behind her.

As she walked to her desk, Gracie turned the envelope over and slipped her thumb through the flap. Expecting a note, she gasped when she saw five hundred-dollar bills. *Then* she saw the note tucked behind the cash. It read, *The thought you put into the gift was enough. Thanks for an unforgettable experience.* It was signed, *Nic.*

Gracie licked the front of her teeth as she stuffed the note and the money back into the envelope. Then she dropped into her chair. She'd given him a gift, and he'd thrown it back in her face. *Why?*

Gracie turned the question over in her brain so many times she had to shake her head to clear it. And then the answer came to her. This was a no-strings affair. It wouldn't last. They'd agreed as much. And a gift of that magnitude was too personal, too familiar, too much for a casual affair like theirs.

When the arrangement was over—and there was no doubt in her mind that he'd move on—he would take a piece of her heart with him. She couldn't stem that hurt, but she could lessen its blow. With this in mind, she devised a plan that would put them back in the casual space he so obviously wanted and she so obviously needed.

Her hands shook as she lifted the receiver and dialed Nic's number.

He answered after one ring. "Gracie?"

"Hi, Nic."

"Was just thinking of you," he said. "I'm having a crappy day and thoughts of you calm me."

Gracie leaned into the receiver as though it would close the distance between them. Ridiculous. This chat was off-script and didn't fit with her plan. "I was wondering if you're available for a drink tonight. I'm heading to New York for the weekend, but I thought it would be nice to see you before I go."

"What time?" he asked.

"Six o'clock?"

Papers rustled in the background, followed by several clicks of the keyboard. "How about seven o'clock? I have a project that I have to finish before then."

"That'll work. Let's meet at the Berkshire Pub on Connecticut. Do you know it?"

"No, but I'll have someone—"

He stopped mid-sentence.

"Nic?"

"Yeah, I'll get the address and meet you there."

"Okay. Let's meet at the bar. Have a better day."

"You already took care of that."

Gracie had no words. A pang of regret made her heart ache.

"Did you receive my delivery?" he asked.

"I did. And the message that came with it. I'll see you tonight."

She didn't wait for his response. Gracie took the receiver and jammed it into the base. Then she picked up the receiver and banged it into the base several more times. With just a few words, he'd undermined her objective—to view him as nothing but the man of the moment. But then she looked down at the envelope on her desk. Well, if Nic wanted casual, that's exactly what he'd get.

CHAPTER TWELVE

The Berkshire Pub bristled with energy. As Ethan scanned the bar, he noticed several men in suits standing together in groups, clinking beers and speaking to each other boisterously. They aimed to relax, to let the stress of the workweek go and just hang. He understood that goal all too well.

The place was small and packed. And nothing like the kind of pub he'd expect Gracie to frequent. The sconces hung on the walls at least ten feet apart and did little to inject the place with either light or cheeriness. And his shoes protested each step along the sticky floor.

A group of women sat at a table near the bar. As he approached the counter, their voices lowered. Ethan nodded at the women and sat on a stool in the center of the bar, turning his head once again to search for Gracie.

Minutes later, he knew without looking that she'd entered the pub. The men to his right continued to talk, but their gazes landed on something behind him, and their boisterous discussion of the upcoming *Sunday Night Football* match-up disinte-grated into vague generalities followed by distracted *uh-uh*s and *yeah*s.

He turned around in his stool. In seconds, he scanned her from head to toe, taking in the slim black skirt that molded to her lithe body, the sheen of gloss on her bow-shaped lips, and the waves of hair that fanned around her. Her absent gaze gutted him—because it skated over the men in the bar as if they were all strangers to her—him included.

He'd play along, but he'd play on his terms. He willed her to look at him simply by the force of his stare. And she did. Then, slowly and purposefully, he turned around and raised his hand to get the bartender's attention.

"Let me have a Wild Turkey, neat, and make it a double," he said.

The bartender nodded and moved away.

Gracie took a stool several feet to his right, away from the clump of men that appeared to be shifting closer to her. She re-moved her trench coat and placed it on the stool beside her. Ethan angled his body in her direction and watched her out of the corner of his eye.

Not surprisingly, one of the men in the clump—a tall, wiry man with shellacked hair and a tailored suit—made his move. Raising the glass of whiskey the bartender placed in front of him, Ethan turned to Gracie with a question in his eyes. She nodded, but he wasn't sure what she'd communicated. *Everything is okay, Ethan. I've got this*? Or: *Come over here and make sure this guy doesn't harass me*?

He waited. And watched. And he ached. Because he wanted to

claim her as his, with a fierceness that made his fingers twitch as they held his drink. She spoke briefly with the man, laughed, and dropped her head. Then her hand lifted several strands of hair and tucked them behind her ear. *Fuck.* She was flirting with the guy? He'd give her two minutes to play out her hand. Nothing more.

The man by Gracie's side moved her trench coat and sat on the stool beside her. Ethan clenched his jaw when the man leaned into her. Playtime was over. Ethan rose from the stool and strode toward the couple that would never be.

Gracie's eyes widened as she watched his approach. Rounding them to stand on Gracie's free side, Ethan set his boot on the bar's foot rail and leaned into her. "I've had enough," he whispered in her ear.

Gracie turned her face in his direction. Her lips, wet and plump, called to him. "Excuse me, do I know you?"

Gracie's companion leaned over. "Is there a problem here?"

Ethan stood and stretched out his chest. "There's no problem. The lady has a choice. I'm asking her to choose me."

The man's eyes flickered between Ethan and Gracie. "Do you know each other?"

Gracie lifted her glass and swirled the red and gold concoction with her straw. Then she took a dainty sip and stared straight ahead. "I don't know him," she replied.

"Dude," the man said to Ethan. "There's a code. You're breaking it."

"*Dude,*" Ethan replied. "I'm more interested in what the lady wants. Can't fault me for that, can you?"

The man took a step back and assessed his competition. Ethan crossed his arms and waited. He hoped his narrow-eyed gaze would be sufficient to chase the man away. He didn't need trouble. Not anymore.

Gracie shifted in her stool and stood between them. "Gentlemen. Let's break this up." Then she turned to Ethan and placed her hands on his chest. "Let's go," she said with a nervous smile.

The man raised his eyebrows and his jaw dropped. "That's it? You're leaving with him?"

Gracie nodded. "That's it. I'm leaving with him. My choice." When she reached for her belongings, Gracie's hands shook. She lifted a few bills from her wallet and set them on the counter. She raised her hand to get the bartender's attention. Pointing between them, she said, "That's for both drinks. His and mine."

She grabbed Ethan's hand and strode toward the pub's exit.

Behind her, Ethan's mind raced. He understood the game, but he didn't understand her motivation. And she hadn't appeared all that comfortable playing it in the first place. Was she trying to prove something to herself? To him? Outside the pub, he stopped walking, causing her to fall back against him because he still held her hand.

"What's going on, Gracie?"

"Nothing, Nic. I was just having a little fun. I thought you'd enjoy it, but I didn't expect you to get into a brawl at a bar."

"That guy wasn't going to fight me."

"Lucky him, I'm sure."

"Exactly."

She again grabbed his hand. "Let's go."

"Where are we going?"

"To my car. It's parked in the lot across the street."

Ethan trailed behind her. Her odd behavior defied explanation. He wished he could get inside that head of hers, but he knew from experience that women were puzzles that couldn't be solved so easily.

* * *

Gracie's heels struck a staccato beat as they hit the pavement, matching the rapid drum of her heart.

Now what?

She'd planned to entice Nic under the guise of anonymity. What man didn't fantasize about having sex with a stranger? *Oh. Right. The man who walked beside her, apparently. He and his furrowed brow could shove it.*

"Let's take the stairs," she said.

They climbed the stairs in silence. The echo of their footsteps grew louder as they approached the door on the second floor. Or maybe that was the pounding of her heart. She had no clue what she'd do when they reached her car. But she needed to act fast. She whipped off her trench coat and folded it over her arm as she trudged up the stairs.

She'd parked her car at the far corner of the lot, hoping it would afford them the privacy they'd need. An hour later, it remained alone in the large space, a significant distance from the cars parked near the stairwell and elevators. The lonely car signaled her intentions like a gaudy neon sign. *Sex in a parking lot, anyone?* the car asked.

She grabbed her key fob from her purse and unlocked her car. "Get in the passenger side," she said. "Give me your jacket."

He angled his head but did as she asked. Then, in silent acknowledgment of her plans for him, he reached for the seat control and pressed it to accommodate his long legs. Gracie threw their jackets in the backseat, and then she climbed in after him. He helped her by raising her skirt as she sat on his lap.

Her Camry was small, and Ethan was large. The cramped quarters heightened her awareness of everything about him.

He squeezed her waist. "We could do this in my bed. It's large and comfortable, and we could roll around in it all night."

"Too tidy," she said. "I want this."

"Are you sure, Gracie? Because we—"

"Nic, please. This is what I want. I don't want to wait. I don't want to think. I just want to feel. It's a simple fuck. It doesn't have to be complicated."

His hands left her sides. "Fine. This is your show. Take it away."

So she did. She unbuttoned his jeans and slid his zipper down. "Rise up," she commanded. When he raised his ass off the seat, she tugged down his jeans and his boxer briefs to his thighs.

His cock sprang to attention and stood stiff as a board. "What are you going to do about your panties?" he whispered.

"Who says I'm wearing any?" she asked as she raised her skirt higher.

Nic's eyes closed on a long moan. "This is the sweetest torture."

She bunched her skirt at the waist and circled her ass on his thighs. "Isn't it, though?"

"Shit, Gracie. You're soaked. Move closer to my cock. I need to feel you there."

She did as he asked. Then she laced her fingers around his neck and leaned in for a kiss. His mouth engulfed hers, the pressure of his lips against hers almost painful. She delighted in it, savoring his tongue. His frenzied exploration of her mouth matched her frenzied undulations against his erection. They engaged in a whirlwind of activity that seemed impossible in the tight space.

Nic's nimble fingers unbuttoned her blouse, and her red satin bra peeked out from the blouse's center. Nic simply stared. She held her breath, wanting him to part the material and reveal her to him. But he did nothing. For a few seconds, her confusion paralyzed her. Then she remembered. *Ah. Right. This was her show.*

Gracie removed her blouse, hitting her elbow on the window in the process. "Ouch," she said.

He clamped down on his bottom lip, stifling a laugh, she was sure, and then he gave her a wry grin. "That bed probably seems more appealing right now, huh?"

She shushed him and lowered the straps of her bra. "Do you want to see them or not?"

"Oh, yes, I'd like to see them."

"Then no more smart comments, Mr. Hill."

Nic's gaze held hers. His green eyes darkened. She was so close she could see when his pupils contracted. She lowered the cups of her bra and her breasts bounced out. "Lick them. Please."

Nic's nostrils flared. Then his head descended to her torso. He drew one nipple into his mouth and licked it in lazy circles. Gracie whimpered. It couldn't be helped. The sound filled the car despite her best effort to stifle it.

The whimper served as Nic's catalyst. After that, his rapid ministrations threatened to overwhelm her. He nipped and sucked on her nipples as his hands outlined the shape of her breasts. And he didn't stop. Over and over, he nipped, sucked, and kneaded.

Gracie shamelessly gyrated on his thigh all the while. Exquisite.

Gracie arched her back and breathed in the scent of their arousal. It was everywhere. She reached for his hard length and held it in her hand. When she slid her hand from the base of his cock to its crown, he stopped moving. She moved her index finger across the crown and slid down to the base. She moved to his ear. "I want this inside me. Now."

He turned his head toward her and captured her mouth. "Take it," he said against it.

"Condom," she said.

He reached in his back pocket and handed her the foil packet.

"You want me to do the honors?" she asked.

"It's your show, remember?"

She opened the packet and rolled the condom down his length. Nic's head hit the headrest. The corded muscles of his neck strained against his smooth skin. She leaned in and sucked on the expanse of skin at his throat. His large hands caressed her back, soothing her despite the flurry of need that wove its way through her.

She couldn't wait any longer. Lifting herself from his thighs, she centered his cock at her entrance. Then she pushed down, reveling in the tight fit. Inch by inch, she took him in. And with each inch, her muscles tightened against him. The friction nearly shattered her.

Nic leaned forward and rested his forehead against the crook of her neck. "Ah, Gracie. It feels incredible. Don't stop, baby."

When she'd taken all of him, she settled in for a long ride. Nic's hands moved from her waist to her backside, kneading the warm flesh. As Gracie rocked into him, Nic met her with his own forceful thrusts. He used his hands to lift her ass, increasing the friction as she slid up and down his cock. Just as she'd planned, Gracie lost herself in the moment.

* * *

Ethan squeezed his eyes shut and gritted his teeth. He expected to explode any minute. But he had to hold on. Had to give Gracie the escape she needed. He opened his eyes and absorbed the image of her rocking into him.

A fine sheen of perspiration covered her skin. Her eyes, glazed and unfocused, drew him in. Her breath hitched, and she began to chant. "Yes, yes, yes. Oh. Right there. Right . . . there."

He reached between them and found her clitoris. Her lips parted. Her eyes, heavy with desire, closed. He stroked her in circles as she continued to ride him.

Hoping to get a better angle, he shifted in the seat and yelped when the seat belt release dug into his hip. "Never again will I let you choose where we hook up."

Her brown eyes widened, and her pupils dilated. "Hook up. Such a perfect description."

She was in a mood, and he wanted to make her come so hard she'd snap out of it. Ethan quickened his thrusts and applied even more pressure to her clit. Gracie's head fell back, and her hair tickled his thighs. "Yes, yes, yes," she cried.

Then her face fell forward. She leaned into him and bit his shoulder. The unexpected sensation threw him. Turned him on in a way that was wholly unfamiliar. "Fuck, yes. Gracie. Bite me, baby. Do what you need."

She sucked on his shoulder instead. He almost stopped when he felt wetness on his shoulders. Was she crying? "What is it?" he asked.

She lifted her head. Her brown eyes seemed to turn black. "Don't stop. Not now."

Seconds later, they came together. His orgasm ripped through his body as she trembled against him, their moans rising and falling until finally an eerie silence remained.

She collapsed against his chest, and he tightened his hold on her waist. The musky air reminded him of the small space and the impromptu nature of this coupling. He didn't know what had brought this on, but he knew with certainty that he'd just experienced one of the most explosive orgasms in all his years. And she didn't even know his real name.

Ethan struggled to reach into his back pocket. "Here," he said as he handed her a handkerchief.

Gracie raised her torso but didn't meet his stare. She took the handkerchief and wiped between her legs. She refused to meet his gaze as she refastened her bra and buttoned her blouse. In silence, she exited the car, kerchief still in hand, and reentered the car on the driver's side. He watched her as she tossed the kerchief on the backseat and retrieved his jacket. Then she handed his jacket to him. Staring straight ahead, she asked, "Do you need a ride somewhere, or did you bring your car?"

Ethan chewed on the inside of his mouth as he righted his clothing. She'd given him the best orgasm of his life, and he wasn't sure he had the strength to leave her car. But he would. Because she obviously wanted him gone.

Maybe she was pissed about the money. "Gracie, if I offended you by sending you the money, I'm sorry. I didn't mean to. It was something I've always wanted to do, so I figured I might as well pay for it. We haven't known each other very long, and that gift was extravagant."

His words cemented the tension in her features. Then, as quickly as her face had tightened, it relaxed, revealing a woman in calm repose. Women. They were inscrutable. Every single one of them.

She inserted a key into the ignition and started the car. "It's okay, Nic. I understand why you sent the money. Ride or not?"

"No ride. I'll catch a cab."

"Okay, great. I have to catch an early train in the morning, so . . ."

"Right. Have a good weekend in New York." He got out of the car and watched her drive away as soon as he'd shut the door.

Then he scratched his head. *What the fuck had just happened?*

CHAPTER THIRTEEN

Gracie wore dark sunglasses during the three-hour train ride to New York. They hid the ginormous bags under her eyes. As if that weren't enough, the headache of the century blasted her temples, and the young man who'd squeezed his way into the window seat wouldn't shut up.

His wrinkled jeans and sweater showed his unfamiliarity with a clothes dryer. And she spied the bag of dirty laundry he'd stuffed into the overhead compartment. College student. Definitely.

"So," he continued. "I'm meeting a few buddies in New York this weekend. It's going to be bananas."

Gracie yawned. "Right."

When her cell phone rang, Gracie grabbed it like it was a life preserver. "Hello?"

"Hey, Graciela," her sister said.

"Hi, Karen. Everything okay?"

"Yes. I just called to warn you. *Papi's* in a mood."

"What now?"

"He called me last night. Oh, Gracie. It was torture." Karen mimicked her father's voice. "*Ay, mis hijas.* My daughters don't call. No one checks on us. They don't visit. Is this any way to treat your parents?"

Gracie grimaced. This was a recurring theme in the Ramirez household. "Thanks for the heads-up."

"Oh, and he asked me about you. Wanted intel on whether you were dating anyone. I told him no. Is that okay?"

An image of last night's rendezvous with Nic flashed across her droopy eyelids. "No, that's fine. I'm not dating anyone."

An unfamiliar silence settled between them. After several seconds, Karen broke it. "Gracie, what's going on?"

Gracie wanted to say something, but the words refused to leave her mouth. What *could* she tell Karen? That she'd agreed to have casual sex with a man? That, despite her best intentions, she wished for more? How could she expect Karen to understand when she didn't understand it herself? "Nothing's going on, sweetie. I'm busy. And I'm going to be stuck with *Papi* for the weekend."

"Oh, no. You're heading to New York this weekend?"

"On the train as we speak. I'll be there in time for lunch."

"Good luck. I told Mom and Dad I'd see them for Christmas. That should hold him off for a month."

Gracie smirked. "Doubt it. But I'm rooting for you anyway. Bye, sweetie."

"*Adios,*" Karen said.

Gracie disconnected the call and shoved her phone in her purse. After last night's debacle, she questioned whether she could continue her arrangement with Nic. Her plan to reestablish the casual connection between them had gone awry. All she'd managed to do was reinforce her suspicion that a casual affair wasn't in her repertoire. She didn't know how to be intimate with someone and remain detached. Yesterday, she'd taken detachment to a dismal level, and had treated Nic poorly in the process.

The young man next to her cleared his throat. "*Papi.* Is that your dad?"

Gracie turned to him and lowered her sunglasses to the bridge of her nose. "Seriously?"

He shrugged his shoulders. "Just trying to pass the time. Want to talk about it?"

"Thanks, but no."

Oddly, she wanted to talk to Nic. He deserved an apology for the dismal way she'd treated him last night. If their roles had been reversed, she would have flattened him with a righteous kick to his groin. Even hours later, her cheeks warmed at the memory of her behavior.

She'd proposed the casual arrangement without much thought. Then she'd convinced herself a no-strings affair would be ideal for her purposes. LTN deserved her undivided attention, she's reasoned, and a serious relationship would distract her. Unfortunately, Nic proved to be a distraction despite their unspoken agreement not to involve their hearts.

Gracie took off her jacket and draped it over her body like a blanket. When in angst, she slept. She settled into her seat, aiming for a nap. With her father's mood in mind, she decided a nap would give her the mental fortification she'd need to get through the weekend. When the weekend was over, she'd decide how to handle her relationship with Nic. Or she'd hibernate for the winter and reemerge in the spring. Yes. That sounded like the perfect plan.

* * *

When Gracie's father opened the door of her childhood home, he greeted her with a wide grin. "Graciela, come in, come in. I was worried you wouldn't be here in time for lunch."

Gracie's stomach rumbled as she slipped out of her jacket. "Made it just in time." She rubbed her hands together and sniffed the air. A familiar and comforting mix of garlic, onion, and coriander filled her nostrils. "Is that *arroz con pollo*?"

Her father nodded. Then he placed Gracie's jacket on a hanger and stuffed it into the hall closet. "It is."

Gracie closed her eyes and pretended to swoon. Her mother's traditional rice with chicken dish was the stuff of legend. "I'll go help."

Her father shuffled after her. "Before you do, go ahead and freshen up. We'll be eating soon."

Gracie's confident stride faltered, and she spun around. "*Papi*, are we expecting someone?"

Her father smiled. "Your mother and I invited Daniel. He should be here any minute. He's in New York for the weekend. We thought it would be nice to see him, and we thought you two might like to see each other, too."

Gracie swallowed and clenched her fists. She should have known her father was up to something. The scoundrel wanted grandbabies, and he wouldn't get them if Gracie didn't marry someone soon. "Daniel's here for the weekend," she said. "Quite a coincidence, wouldn't you say?"

Her father scratched the back of his head and refused to meet her hard gaze. "I might have mentioned that you'd be here."

Gracie's ears burned at the thought that her dad had tried to play matchmaker. "*Papi*, just stop. Daniel and I aren't going to fall in love and get married. You're wasting your time."

Her father crossed his arms, a sure sign he was prepared to duke it out. "Graciela, he's a good man. He's smart, makes good money, and he likes you. What's wrong with dating him? Maybe you'd grow to love him."

Gracie pursed her lips. "I'd have to learn to like him first."

"Be nice, Graciela. We taught you better than that."

"Sorry, you're right. But that doesn't change the fact that I'm not interested in Daniel."

"Well, you need to get interested in someone soon, Graciela. You're not getting younger. And you're spending too much time on work. You need balance."

"For goodness' sake, *Papi*. I'm twenty-seven, hardly a candidate for a nursing home. And there's nothing wrong with focusing on work."

"Work isn't going to keep you warm at night."

"And a cheating husband isn't going to keep me warm at night, either."

"Enough," her father said. The sharp edge to his voice was followed by a deep sigh. "There are good men out there. Men who don't lie. Men who don't cheat. You're looking at one right now. If you don't want to date Daniel, fine. I can't make you. But don't swear off men because you're so focused on your career. You'll only be hurting yourself in the end."

Then he turned and trudged up the stairs. She refused to go after him. First off, she didn't avoid men. Exhibit A, in the form of a sexy computer consultant with piercing green eyes, came to mind. And her preoccupation with work warranted praise, not censure. This constant push and pull between them exhausted her. Was it any wonder she didn't visit more often?

She waltzed into the kitchen, acting as if that uncomfortable exchange with her father hadn't happened. Her mother, lovely as ever, danced to the salsa music playing from a small radio on the kitchen counter. Lydia Ramirez wore slacks and a billowy top that didn't mesh with the soiled kitchen towel draped over her shoulder or the sauce-splattered oven mitts covering her hands. Gracie imagined her mother had gotten dressed for brunch in Manhattan, thought better of it, and decided to cook instead.

She planted a kiss on her mother's cheek. "*Hola, Mami.*"

"Hi, Graciela. Giving your father a hard time as usual."

"You heard?"

"I hear everything, sweetheart."

"Well, then you know why I gave him a hard time. He won't quit meddling."

Her mother laughed as she stirred the pot of rice and chicken. "That's what fathers do, Graciela. Mothers, too. But your father's so good at it, I let him do it all on his own."

Gracie groaned. "Tell me you don't approve of his plan to get me hitched to Daniel."

"I don't approve, but there's no point in saying so. Daniel's not the man for you. I know it. You know it. Your father will know it, too. Eventually. Just get through the lunch."

Gracie riffled through the utensil drawer, found a spoon, and sidled up to the steaming pot. "Taste, please?"

"Just one, and then please finish fixing the table," her mother said.

Gracie scooped a spoonful of the dish and placed it in her mouth. The dish packed just enough heat to make her tongue tingle. "So good," she murmured as she placed the spoon in the sink.

The doorbell rang. Gracie's raised her head to the ceiling and let out an exaggerated groan. Her mother, meanwhile, flitted around the kitchen as though she hadn't heard the doorbell at all.

"I guess I'll get it," Gracie said.

She stomped to the door and flung it open. "Fancy meeting you here, Daniel. What brings you to town?"

Daniel ignored her sarcasm. "Hi, Graciela. As always, it's a pleasure." He held a bouquet of fall flowers in his hand.

Gracie reached for them. "You shouldn't have."

Daniel swatted her hand away and grinned. "I didn't. These are for your mother."

Gracie closed her mouth and ushered him in. "Can I get your jacket?"

"Yes, thanks."

As she took his jacket, Gracie's father sauntered down the stairs. "Daniel, so good to see you."

"Hector, likewise. How are the Giants treating you this season?"

"Same as always, Daniel. Always so close. Just enough to make an old man hope, but not enough to make me win the pool at the job."

Daniel pulled his phone from his back pocket. "I went to Cozumel a few weeks ago. Deep-sea diving like you wouldn't believe. Let me show you pictures."

Daniel and her father viewed pictures on Daniel's phone as they made their way to the couch. Gracie watched them interact as she hung his jacket on a hook in the hall. If she were the kind of woman who put her father's wishes above her own needs, she and Daniel would have dated years ago. But Daniel didn't steal her breath when he walked into a room. She didn't squirm when his heated gaze roved over her body. And she didn't look forward to seeing him, if only for a few minutes during the week. No, she reserved those reactions for Nic.

Her mother breezed into the living room. "Hi, Daniel."

As usual, Daniel charmed her mother with his wide smile. "Hi, Mrs. Ramirez." He made a dramatic show of presenting her with the bouquet.

"Thank you, Daniel. They're beautiful." Lydia Ramirez looked at her husband as she sniffed the flowers. "Hector, I need your help in the kitchen."

Her father looked up. With a slight narrowing of her eyes, Gracie's mother told her father it was time to haul his butt to the kitchen. Before her mother breezed out of the room, she directed a pointed stare to Gracie. "Tell him," her mother mouthed.

Yes, she supposed she could use a few minutes to undo her father's machinations and make clear to Daniel she only wanted his friendship. She crossed the room and sat next to him.

Daniel continued to swipe his finger across his phone, shuffling through the pictures of his deep-sea diving adventure. "Want to check them out?"

Gracie reined in her annoyance, reminding herself that Daniel wasn't the villain here. "I'd love to. But later. Can we talk about what's going on here?"

Daniel set his phone on the coffee table. "Your father, you mean."

"Yes, my father. I know he means well, but you and I know this isn't going to go anywhere."

"We do?"

"Yes, yes, we do. We're friends, Daniel. Or at least I'd like us to be. And we would be if I didn't feel uncomfortable around you."

Daniel drew away from her and regarded her with round eyes. "I make you uncomfortable?"

"Daniel, when a woman says she isn't interested, that should be the end of it."

"But what if she's playing hard to get?"

"I can't speak for most women, but I'm not playing hard to get. And you should err on the side of assuming a woman means what she says. These *can't* be new concepts to you."

A flush spread across Daniel's cheeks and he dipped his chin. Oh, my goodness. These *were* new concepts to him. Gracie clasped her hands between her knees. Now she understood why she appealed to Daniel: She said no to him, and that anomaly held his interest.

After several seconds of silence, Daniel raised his chin and stared at her. "Okay. Got it. You're not interested." He rose from the couch and faced her, extending his hand. "Friends?"

She took his hand and stood. "Friends."

"What are you going to do about your father?"

"You mean the mule in the kitchen? Nothing. Eventually he'll realize that my career comes first, whether or not he approves. I won't let him force me into a relationship."

Gracie's mother called them into the dining room. Daniel motioned for her to proceed him. "Why can't you have both?"

Gracie recalled her missed meeting with the president of the Bentley Foundation. "Because one of them will always suffer."

She'd been distracted by Nic the day she missed that appointment. Caught up in spending time with him. In bed. Had she thought she could carry on an affair with Nic and not become distracted? The idea made her laugh inside.

LTN needed her undivided attention. Trying to navigate a no-strings relationship with Nic took more effort than she could give to the task. And the role she'd played in that car—treating him as nothing more than a sex object worthy of a quickie and a ride home—was her worst performance yet. She'd been on the receiving end of such treatment with Neal. Unlike Neal, she wasn't able to do justice to the role, nor did she want to.

The answer to her quandary was clear: It was time to end the affair.

CHAPTER FOURTEEN

The ding of his iPhone startled Ethan out of a fitful sleep. Reaching for the phone, he paused when his torso connected with the empty space next to him. Graciela should have been there. Instead, she was in New York.

He squinted at the phone and saw that she'd sent him a text:

Would you mind meeting me at the coffee shop on Kalorama at 4?

Shouldn't take long. G.

Ethan dropped the phone on the night table and settled on the bed. Fuck. She was going to cut him off. And he knew why. Gracie had offered him a casual arrangement, and he'd agreed to it without much thought as to whether it was in her best interests. From the beginning, she'd pretended to want what he wanted—a casual affair.

True, her father had conditioned her to believe that a committed relationship would threaten her professional goals, would make her lose her focus. And Ethan had seized on that belief to justify being with her. But Gracie clashed with her father because they disagreed on a fundamental point: a woman's ability to successfully manage a career and a family. Gracie didn't see it yet, but she longed for a serious commitment, and what she and Ethan shared was anything but serious.

Now that the end of their relationship loomed, Ethan wondered whether he was capable of giving her more. But giving her more would mean he'd have to reveal his true identity, and although in the grand scheme of things his identity didn't mean much, the fact that he'd lied to her would mean a lot.

He didn't deserve her, but he wanted her nonetheless.

Yes, the pleasure of being inside her floored him. But he was prepared to admit that the pleasure was rooted in the connection he felt to her as a person, as a friend. She comforted him, made him laugh, and pushed him to think beyond his typical assumptions. Her observation that he was running from something still shocked him. Because it was true. And he hadn't absorbed that truth until Gracie forced him to.

Could he face her disapproval when he told her the truth? If he wanted to be with her, there was no other option. And what did he have to lose anyway? Because if he didn't do something, she would cut him off this afternoon. He was man enough to admit that he didn't want to stop seeing her. No, he wanted more, not less.

But he'd have to go about it carefully. He would convince her that he was committed to being in a steady relationship. *Then* he would share his history with her and explain his reasons for withholding a part of himself. His reasons had nothing to do with her and everything to do with his circumstances. She'd understand, wouldn't she? He'd make sure of it.

But first, the fun part: convincing her that he was all in. Ethan scratched his chin, waiting for a brilliant idea to materialize. Unfortunately, nothing came to him. His eyes darted around his bedroom and landed on an empty take-out carton resting on his nightstand. An idea formed. Brilliant. Just brilliant. He texted Gracie a single word in response: *Okay*. Then he jumped out of bed, eager to put his plan into action. It was time to go shopping.

* * *

Carrying two heavy shopping bags, Ethan struggled into the vestibule of Gracie's multi-apartment brownstone. He dropped the bags on the floor and entered the three-digit code to buzz her apartment.

"Yes?" she asked.

"Gracie, it's Nic. Can you buzz me up?"

Her muffled response crackled through the intercom speaker. "Sure. C'mon up."

When he reached the second-floor landing, Gracie waited at the door. She wore leggings, a long sweater, and wool socks that slouched around her ankles. Her face bore no hint of makeup, and her hair was tied in a high ponytail.

Her eyebrows rose in surprise when her gaze landed on the shopping bags in his hands. "Hi. What's all this?"

Ethan's clammy hands caused him to lose his grip on one of the shopping bags. What the hell was wrong with him? He fumbled to recover the bag and moved closer to her. "Could I explain inside?"

Gracie stepped back and swung the door open. "Of course. Sorry."

He followed her into the living room and noticed the half-full glass of wine on her coffee table. "Rough weekend?"

Her high-pitched laugh ended with a sigh. "Not at all."

He raised an eyebrow and waited.

She dropped onto the couch and tucked her legs under her. "You're right. I didn't have a great time. My dad arranged for a suitor to join us for lunch on Saturday."

Ethan's stomach dropped. Did she plan to cut him off so she could date this guy? He set the bags on the floor and sat next to her. He clenched and unclenched his fists, pretending to warm himself after braving the biting November wind. "How'd that turn out?"

"It was uncomfortable. He's a friend of the family. His parents and my parents, I mean. My father would love for us to get together. My mother, thank goodness, is on my side. I made it clear to Daniel that it wasn't going to happen. But I was annoyed I had to have that conversation to begin with. Needless to say, I wasn't pleased with my father's shenanigans." She clapped her hands, signaling the end of that part of the conversation. "So anyway. I'm dying to know the deal with the bags."

Ethan leaned forward and placed his elbows on his knees. She untucked her legs and leaned forward, matching his pose. "What is it?" she asked as she nudged his knee with her own.

Ethan straightened and turned toward her. "I want to cook dinner for you."

Gracie drew back and scanned him from head to toe. "Are you sure? Because you look like you're being walked to the gallows. Is your cooking *that* bad?"

Ethan dropped his head and laughed. "I'm doing this wrong." He reached for her hands, placed them on his thighs, and covered her hands with his. "I want to be the man who gets to cook for you. More than once." His voice broke on those last few words.

Gracie moved her hands and pressed them between her thighs. "We were supposed to meet later today. So I could end this. Nothing dramatic. Just a simple explanation that our arrangement is more than I want to handle right now."

"I know."

She jerked back. "How'd you know?"

"The car."

"The car?"

"Yeah. I knew something was wrong when we fucked in the car."

Gracie flinched at his words. "Way to change the tone of this conversation, Mr. Romance."

He dragged a hand through his hair and cracked his neck, appearing frustrated and then unaffected in the space of a few seconds. "I came here to ask for a commitment. Forgive me if it isn't coming out like a sonnet. I want to be with you. It's that simple. If it's not what you want, just tell me and I'll go."

Ethan held his breath. Maybe she genuinely didn't want to be in a committed relationship. Maybe he'd miscalculated the extent of her feelings for him. Her furrowed brow certainly suggested that she was torn. What the hell was she contemplating over there?

"Please don't misunderstand. I appreciate all this," she said as she waved her hands in the direction of the shopping bags. "But I've got a lot going on right now." She stood and wrapped her arms over her middle. "LTN's future is bleak. If I don't turn things around, I'll be headed to New York by start of the fiscal year."

The possibility that she'd leave the city had never entered his mind. "Which is when?"

"March first of next year. I just don't think it's wise to get serious about anyone under the circumstances. I have to focus on LTN. I hope you can understand."

What could he say really? If he said he didn't understand, she'd think he didn't understand the pressure she was under. And he understood it all too well. He searched for something to say that would change her mind about them, but the rigid set of her jaw warned him away. "I can respect that. I guess I'll go then. Keep the bags. There's nothing fancy in there. Spaghetti and meatballs, an old family favorite."

She nodded.

He studied her for any sign that she didn't want him to leave. Hoped she'd call him back. As he neared her door, his hope diminished. His hand wrapped around the doorknob at the same time her finger tapped him on the shoulder.

He spun to face her. "Yeah?"

"Stay. We could make dinner together."

Right. She'd just ditched him. Hanging around would make him bleed out. *Thanks, but no thanks.* "That's okay, Gracie. I think I should head home."

She held her hand out to him. "Friends?"

Sure, he'd be professional about it, but friends? Was she serious? He couldn't be her friend, not when he longed to plunge inside her and make her shout his name. Not when he wanted to talk to her in the afterglow of great sex. Not when he wanted to brand her as his woman. Not when he wanted to wake up to her warm smile. It would be too hard.

Surely this was payback for what he'd done. Remembering he was a good liar who didn't deserve her anyway, he grasped her hand and gave it a firm shake. "Friends, it is. See you next week."

He shouldn't have sought her out in the first place. There were literally hundreds of community service organizations where he could have completed his service hours. But he'd led with his dick, lost his heart along the way, and now he was fucked.

Not so nice to meet you, Karma.

CHAPTER FIFTEEN

For several weeks, Gracie barricaded herself in her office when Nic visited LTN. She'd pop out to say hello and then scurry back to her office. She spent most of her days fielding phone calls from potential donors, updating the board on any leads, and devising alternative sources of funding.

They'd talked a few times, about superficial matters—the weather, their respective plans for the holidays, and Calliope's antics. Each time, though, she yearned to run her fingers through his hair and draw him in for a searing kiss. She wished she could trust herself to be with him, to enjoy his company without losing herself in him. But given the roller coaster she'd ridden during their brief affair, Gracie knew he'd consume her.

She needed a weekend in bed, with a book and hot cocoa for company. Instead, she was scheduled to attend a charity awards dinner at Mimi's request. If it weren't for Mimi's observation that she could use the event to promote LTN, Gracie would have declined. Now she needed a dress and would have to brave the holiday crowds to find one.

Gracie shut down her desktop. As she gathered her personal belongings, Nic's familiar form filled her office doorway.

Gracie steeled herself against the attraction that continued to bind them. He watched her, saying nothing. How was she supposed to look at him and not remember his touch, his kisses, the pleasure she'd experienced at his hands?

He looked no different than usual. His mouth, however, was set in a firm line that warned her she might not appreciate what he had to say. "Duty calls, but I wanted to give you something before I left. May I come in?"

"Of course."

He stepped back and reached for an object on the floor outside her office. When he moved through the doorway, he held a wrapped box in his hands. "It's a gift. I purchased it before . . ."

Gracie stood and reached for the box. "Thank you, but you didn't have—"

His nostrils flared. "I know I didn't *have* to. I wanted to." He lifted his face to the ceiling and ran a hand through the back of his hair. "I just wanted you to know that you meant something to me. I thought you'd like this."

He was close, watching her with wariness in his eyes. Gracie smiled as her heart thudded in her chest. This was what he did to her. Made her forget where she was. Made her vibrate with need until she thought she would burst. She relaxed her features and ventured an unaffected response. "Should I open it now?"

"Sure."

The giftwrap was exquisite. A gold foil tied with a silky dark blue bow. Underneath, a nondescript box shrouded his gift in mystery. She opened the box, peeked inside, and pulled out a small statue. A reproduction of Degas's famous sculpture. *La Petite Danseuse de Quatorze Ans. Little Dancer Aged Fourteen.*

The shield around Gracie's heart cracked. If Nic were quick enough, he might be able to fight his way inside. "It's lovely, Nic." After studying the statue at length, she said, "There's something about her pose, face tilted upward as if she's relieved, her long legs out of position. That statue has always stirred something in me. A young woman forced to be someone she doesn't want to be. It's always intrigued me. And I can see now that it reminds me of you."

He stepped closer to her. "Is that what you see?"

His voice was so low she could barely hear it. Her gaze fell to his lips and an image of her tugging on them with her own flashed in her brain. "Yes."

"Gracie, what do you see when you look at me?"

Gracie swallowed and set the sculpture on her desk. "I see a man."

"What else?"

"I see a man who's tired, burdened by something."

Nic stepped closer to her, close enough to permit her to feel the warmth radiating from his body. "What do you see now?"

Gracie's torso inched closer to him, but she pressed her toes against the bottom of her shoes, desperately needing an anchor. "I see a man who wants me."

"Gracie, I want you so much it hurts." He reached out and took her hand, lifting it to his lips. "Here." To his crotch. "Here."

To his heart. "And most of all, here." He moved a few strands of hair away from her face. "Give us a chance. Please."

Gracie couldn't resist him. Decided it was foolish to try. But she had no idea what kind of chance he was asking for. "What do you want exactly?"

"I want to be your lover. For as long as you'll have me."

"What if things don't work out with LTN and I have to return to New York? What then?"

"I have confidence in you. You'll find a way to keep LTN's doors open. I'm sure of it. But if not, we'll deal with it. Somehow." Nic's knuckles grazed her cheek. "I want to be with you. It's that simple."

Gracie wanted him to envelop her in his arms. She wanted to be swept away by him. Wanted to trust that he meant every word. "Okay."

He raised his eyebrows and regarded her with wide eyes. "Okay?"

"Yes."

He smiled. "Okay." He looked around him as though he hadn't expected her to acquiesce. She grabbed his chin and rose to meet his lips. Back in his element, he fused his lips with hers and pressed her back until her butt hit her desk. He rested his hands on her desk, caging her with his body, with his heat. His lips moved from her mouth to her neck and Gracie's core ached for his touch.

A wretched text tone sounded from his cell phone. It figured they would be interrupted. Gracie tried to place the melody. "'Bad to the Bone'? That's your text tone?"

He rested his forehead against hers. "Not my idea. My sister

Emily changed it the last time I was home. I didn't bother to change it back." He pulled his phone out of his back pocket and stared at the screen. "It's Mark. Work interferes again. Listen, I have a work event this evening, but I'd like to see you later tonight. We need to talk."

"Talk? Right."

"Yes, talk." He wiggled his eyebrows. "What happens after that is up to you."

"Sure. I'll text you when I get home."

"Okay." He pressed a soft kiss to her lips and stepped back.

"Have a nice evening, Nic."

"I'll be thinking about you, Gracie." He spun toward the door and strode out of her office, giving her a final glimpse at his tantalizing backside. Some men were made to wear jeans that sat low on their hips and hugged their thighs. Nic was one of them.

She shook her head and took a deep breath. Nic *wanted* to be with her. He wanted to be hers, he'd said. So she was going to give him the chance she asked for. And she wouldn't lose sight of her priorities in the process. She could have it all, couldn't she?

Suddenly, tonight's awards dinner didn't seem as ominous. Probably because she had a weekend with Nic to look forward to. The sooner the dinner ended, the sooner she could enjoy her time with Nic.

CHAPTER SIXTEEN

Gracie slipped through the doors of the Newseum and searched for signs to the Blakely Awards Dinner. Mimi was right. The dinner would be an appropriate place to begin touting LTN as an organization worthy of donor support. She would mingle with the guests and talk up LTN whenever possible.

She wished Nic were here with her. Nic. He was addictive. Even now she would have preferred to be in his bed, wrapped in his arms. She had to remember, though, that LTN came first. Her clients needed her, and if she had to spend time away from Nic to save LTN, she would. No question.

She followed the signs to the awards dinner and entered a stately atrium with a jaw-dropping glass roof. Guests stood in small groups, laughing and talking, while others waited in line to order a drink. Good idea. She needed liquid courage. She was comfortable in social situations, but she preferred to be out of the spotlight. Talking up LTN would require her to grab the attention of strangers. A glass of wine would relax her.

As she waited in line, a familiar voice whispered in her ear. "Lovely to see you, Graciela. You look beautiful tonight."

Gracie smiled, genuinely happy to see Daniel. "Good evening, Daniel. How are you?"

"Great, now that you're here. Are you alone?"

He was handsome. She'd give him that. Daniel was refined and suave. He worked at it, and it showed. Nic, on the other hand, was comfortable in his own skin. He owned who he was. And he didn't need to put on airs. He was a formidable man. Intelligent. Charming. Strong. Although Daniel possessed many of those qualities, he always seemed to be working at it, whereas, for Nic, those qualities came naturally to him.

"Mimi's here," she told Daniel. "She's working, though. I'll be sitting at her table once I find it."

She moved to the bar counter when it was her turn. "Do you have a Sauvignon Blanc?" she asked the bartender.

He nodded and poured her a glass.

"I'll have the same," Daniel told him.

When they'd received their wine, they moved away from the bar. Her gaze swept the room. Then the lights flickered. "Daniel, I'm going to find my table. Maybe I'll see you later?"

"Sure. Save a dance for me."

Gracie gave him a noncommittal nod and headed toward the double doors of the ballroom. After she located her place card, she smiled at the young man who handed her a program. He was smartly dressed in a tuxedo. "You look nice," she told him.

The young man blushed. "Thank you."

Gracie laughed as she wove her way through the tables to find her own. The evening would be a success. She'd make sure of it.

She'd just found her table when Mimi brushed against her.

"Gracie, goodness. You look remarkable."

Gracie twirled so Mimi could get the full effect of the dress, a one-shouldered red silk gown reminiscent of the glamorous styles Hollywood starlets had made famous in the forties. Gracie's hair, which she'd curled into loose waves, complemented the dress. "You like?"

"Like?" Mimi asked. "I love."

"You look stunning, too," Gracie said. And it was true. Mimi's blond hair was pulled into a stylish chignon, highlighting her elegant neckline. Pearl teardrop earrings were her only accessory. And the black dress, complete with an embroidered bustier, emphasized her sleek physique.

Mimi's eyes lit up. "Ah. This old thing. I just threw on whatever was in my closet."

Gracie laughed. "Right."

Mimi snorted. "I owe you one for being my plus one. C'mon, let's sit."

"Okay."

Mimi immediately struck up a conversation with a gentleman to her left while Gracie studied the program. The awards dinner honored individuals and companies that had made significant contributions to the Blakely Fund, which in turn donated money to literacy programs around the country. Mimi was the Fund's publicist, hence the reason Gracie was able to snag an invitation to the exclusive dinner.

Media Best was one of the companies being honored. According to the program, Media Best was a leader in Internet software and technologies. She wasn't familiar with the company and didn't recall seeing it on the list Nic had prepared. She circled the name and made a mental note to look into the company this weekend.

Thirty minutes later, Gracie talked with a woman seated next to her. The woman was the vice president of a local bank and expressed interest in LTN's mission.

Mimi tugged her arm. "The honors are about to be handed out," she said. "The person accepting for Media Best is not to be missed." Then Mimi fanned herself.

Ah, man candy.

"How do you know?" Gracie asked.

"It's my job to know, remember? This guy's the CEO of Media Best. Champion of all causes. A man with a bad boy streak and a guilty heart. And he's not a big fan of being in the limelight, so this is a rare treat. You need to hit him up for a donation."

Gracie took a sip of her wine and turned toward the stage. Mimi's description had sparked her attention. The emcee read a description of Media Best's interests and its contributions to the Blakely Fund. Impressive. She'd definitely research the company this weekend.

"Accepting on behalf of Media Best is Ethan Hill," the emcee said as he encouraged the crowd to clap with him.

Gracie's soft clap ended with a gasp. Attempting to reach for her wineglass for fortitude, she knocked it over instead. Her neighbor rose to avoid getting the spilled wine on her dress, and all eyes, including Nic's, searched for the source of the commotion.

Gracie apologized, and a waiter swept in to clear the mess. Gracie just sat there. Nic was on the stage. In a tuxedo. That alone confused her, because it was so different from his typical jeans and plaid shirt or sweater, which she'd come to think of as his staple wardrobe. Her brain failed her, unable to connect the moving parts that jumbled in her head. She shook her head as though doing so would help clarify what her mind was unable to process.

Mimi leaned toward her. "What's wrong?"

"I know him."

Mimi's eyebrows shot up. "You do?"

Gracie's heart raced, and her stomach rumbled. She had no idea what game he'd been playing, but she knew she'd been duped. By Nic. Ethan. Whatever the hell his name was. "I do. That's Nic."

Mimi's eyes widened, and a hand flew to her mouth. "Ethan is Nic? Nic is Ethan?"

"Yes."

"Oh, Gracie. I'm sorry. There has to be some reasonable explanation, though."

Her brain flashed an image of the paperwork his lawyer had submitted with the court's brochure about the community service program. Ethan had been identified as Nicholas E. Hill. He hadn't misrepresented himself, but he hadn't been entirely forthcoming, either. "There's an explanation, but it's not reasonable. I guarantee it."

"What are you going to do?"

An excellent question to which she had no answer. She took a deep breath as she tried to make sense of it all. And piece by piece disparate parts of the puzzle came together to form a whole. His initial resistance to being in a relationship with her now made sense. His presence at the Kennedy Center to "fulfill an obligation" now made sense. The man on stage today bore a striking resemblance to the stranger she'd seen that evening. She hadn't known it then, but Nic, not Ethan, had been the impostor all along.

She winced as she remembered the stupid deal they'd negotiated. Of course, he'd been all in after that. And why not? She'd given him a free pass to walk away after their affair was over. She'd offered him the perfect arrangement: sex without the inconvenience of strings. No hard feelings, she'd promised. No drama, she'd said. To hell with that.

Gracie's eyes narrowed. "I'm going to confront him."

Mimi laughed. "There's the fire. This is why we're best friends. What can I do to help?"

"I'm not going to confront him just yet. Could you use your feminine powers of persuasion to get the band to play 'At Last'?"

Mimi nodded. "Okay, then. I'll do that and come back here to watch the show."

"You do that. I'm going to the restroom to freshen up. Be back soon."

As she fled, Gracie tried to shut out the sound of the audience's applause. Yes, he should take a bow. His Oscar-worthy performance certainly had fooled her.

* * *

In the restroom, Gracie paced. She wanted to cry, but a mussed look wouldn't be appropriate for what she had in mind. What possible reason could he have had to lie to her? They'd made love numerous times. She'd opened up to him about her insecurities, about her job, about her father's long-standing disapproval of her desire to be a professional in her own right.

She grabbed a tissue and blew her nose. He'd shared his thoughts, his views on politics, and bits and pieces about his family life. But she knew now that he was holding back the most important piece of information about himself: who he really was.

She was a fool. A fool who'd almost fallen in love with him. A fool who was paying for her lapse in judgment yet again. Hadn't she learned anything from her experience with Neal? She didn't need any more heartache to get the message: Your career will always be there for you, but a man most certainly will let you down. Okay. She finally got it. Yes, she'd move on, and she'd view the man out there as an unfortunate mistake, set aside her time with … Nic … Ethan … She didn't know what to call him. *Shit.*

She grabbed the compact from her clutch and freshened her makeup. With a soft pop of her newly glossed lips, she stormed out of the restroom. Then she searched for Daniel.

She found him within minutes. He was standing at the outskirts of the dance floor, surrounded by a gaggle of women laughing with him. She didn't bother to be polite. She simply walked up to him and grabbed his hand. "Sorry, ladies. I need to steal him for a minute."

Daniel gaped at her, but he recovered quickly and assumed the commanding pose of the debonair bachelor he purported to be—chest out, legs locked, hands in his pockets. "What's going on, Gracie?"

"Look, we're just friends, right?"

Daniel chuckled. "Yep. You made that clear in New York."

"Okay. Well, now I need your help. I want to make someone

jealous. I figure you might be up to the task. But I didn't want to confuse you with this charade."

"No worries, Gracie. I know it's never going to happen between us."

She breathed a sigh of relief. She'd gotten through to him, thank goodness. "Okay."

Daniel nodded. "Okay. So what do you need me to do?"

"I need you to act like we're together. Dance with me. Nothing overt. I don't want to make a bad impression with potential colleagues. But something that will stake a claim."

Daniel's lifted an eyebrow. "Mixed signals, much?"

"Daniel."

Daniel sobered and jammed his hands in his pockets. "Okay, okay. I'll do it. This should be fun."

Gracie smirked. He wasn't bad at all.

With an elegant flourish, he threaded his fingers through hers. "Shall we dance?"

Gracie aimed a playful smile in his direction. "I thought you'd never ask."

Daniel swept her on to the dance floor. On Mimi's cue, the band began to play Etta James's 'At Last.' The song was perfect. Daniel wrapped her in his arms, and she laid her head on his shoulder. She squirmed, though, when he began to rub her back.

"Too much?" he whispered.

"No, it's fine. But if you touch my butt, I will knee you in the nuts."

"Not the nicest thing to say to a man who's helping you out. What about a kiss on the jaw. Would that work?"

"A quick one. No need to overdo it."

"Got it."

She lifted her head and stared into his eyes. She felt *nothing*. And she cursed Ethan for making her feel *something*. Everything. Too much.

Daniel bent his head and kissed her jaw. Instinct compelled her to close her eyes.

A voice behind her cleared his throat. She turned and there he was. Nic. Ethan. The reminder that she'd been calling him by another name—in bed, too—incensed her. The tension in his jaw mirrored the tension between them. His eyes flashed in anger. Was she supposed to understand the reason for his deceit from that look alone? She thought not. She wasn't the one in the wrong here, but his clenched jaw suggested he thought otherwise. Damn him.

Gracie wanted to run, but she stood her ground. She refused to reveal how much he'd hurt her. She edged closer to Daniel and linked her arm with his. Ethan's gaze darted from their linked arms to her face.

Somehow she managed to pretend his revelation hadn't shocked her. "Mr. Hill, congratulations," she said. "Your company's charitable contributions are impressive."

He relaxed the squint in his eyes and held out his hand. "May I speak with you, Gracie?"

She ignored his hand and lifted her chin a notch. "I don't think so, Mr. Hill. I don't know you very well, do I?"

His head whipped back as though she'd sucker-punched him. Lips pressed tightly together, he dropped his outstretched hand. "Fine. I'll follow up with you soon. This isn't the place. But we *will* talk."

Daniel grabbed her hand, raised it to his mouth, and kissed it. "C'mon, Graciela. Let's head out. I'd like to get you away from here."

Ethan's jaw froze, and the hands at his sides clenched into fists. He stepped close to Daniel and ground out his words in a scratchy tone. "She's mine, whether she knows it or not. There will be no scraps, no leftovers, no nothing. There's nothing left of her she could give you. *I* have it all. She knows it. I know it. You should know it, too."

What the hell? When had she morphed into a piece of beef jerky? In that moment, she hated him. She hated him so much her body trembled from his proximity. "Okay, that's enough," she said to Ethan. With a practiced smile, she turned to Daniel. "Let's go."

Daniel shrugged his shoulders and sneered at Ethan. "The lady has spoken." Then he draped his arm around Gracie's shoulders and led her to the doors of the ballroom.

As she and Daniel walked away, Daniel whispered, "Is that what you needed?"

"Yes, that was perfect. Thanks."

Daniel followed her out the door, his comforting hand resting lightly on her back. Gracie took several steps and paid no attention to her surroundings. Instead, she recalled the tick in Ethan's jaw and marveled at the man's gall. He'd hidden his role at Media Best. It was bad enough that he'd hidden such an important part of his life from her. But she suspected there was more to the story, a reason he didn't want her to know about his connection to the company.

Yes, they'd talk. But they'd do it on her terms. And her terms required her to sob in private, until she could face him without any emotion. She planned to wring her eyes dry of any tears, so she could excise him out of her life forever without him knowing how much he'd hurt her.

She reached into her clutch for her phone, but Mimi was right behind her.

"Need to stay at my place for the weekend?" Mimi asked.

Gracie's heart swelled. Ethan's betrayal made her appreciate Mimi's loyalty more than ever. "Yes," she whispered as she wiped away a tear.

Mimi hugged her. Then Mimi turned to Daniel. "I've got it from here, Daniel."

The light in Daniel's eyes dimmed. "Fine," he said to Mimi. "Take care, Gracie. Hope you're okay." He strode away.

Shielding Gracie from inquiring eyes that noticed the distress on her face, Mimi led her to the elevator that would take her away from the travesty of this night.

CHAPTER SEVENTEEN

The Monday after the charity awards fiasco, Ethan stood outside LTN's doors, checking his watch. The wind howled, and the force of it against his cheeks chased away his lingering grogginess. He hadn't slept well over the weekend. When he tried, the disappointment that flashed across Gracie's face would appear in his dreams and stir him to wake.

Where was she?

She'd ignored the voice mail messages he'd left her over the weekend. She'd ignored his insistent banging on her apartment door. But she couldn't ignore him here.

Before his evening had turned to shit on Friday, Ethan had planned to tell Gracie everything. He'd known she'd be angry, but he'd hoped she would come to understand the reasons for his deception.

Unfortunately, his chance to volunteer that information had evaporated the minute she'd seen him on that stage. He'd smiled for the cameras, accepted the award on behalf of Media Best, and thanked the audience for its support of the company's charitable endeavors. All the while, Gracie had been in that audience, shocked by the revelation that the man she was dating was Ethan Hill, CEO of Media Best. Ethan couldn't fault her for being angry.

Ethan leaned on the door and rested his head against it. She might not forgive him. Then what? He'd plead, grovel, and beg for her forgiveness. And he'd convince her that he was committed to being a permanent fixture in her life.

Minutes passed. Still there was no sign of her. He cupped his hands and blew on them, inwardly cursing the bite of the December wind. Then Gracie's lithe form appeared. He watched her approach. His heart thumped a steady drum against his chest, and his stomach muscles tightened. She wore large, black-framed sunglasses, a red three-quarter-length trench coat, and a frown that suggested she wanted to squeeze his balls until he sang like a soprano.

He pushed off the door and gave her space to pass.

She didn't acknowledge his presence. Instead, she opened the alarm panel and entered her entry code. The lock on the door clicked, and then she swung the door open and slipped inside.

He'd just closed the door behind him when she rounded on him. "What the hell are you doing here?"

"I called. All weekend. You didn't answer. This was the only way."

She rolled her eyes, turned around, and stomped toward her office.

This wouldn't be easy.

* * *

Gracie wanted to feed her anger. Ratchet up her annoyance. Throw something at him. A vase. A stapler. Anything. She wanted her anger to fester, because she didn't want to cry in his presence. Not over him.

She struggled out of her trench and threw it on the guest chair. Behind her, his footsteps slowed. The click of the door assured them of privacy. She turned around and surveyed him, taking in his motionless form, the rigid set of his jaw, and the eyes that refused to gaze in her direction. With his shoulders lowered and his hands in his back pockets, his broad chest emerged as his dominant physical feature. She'd laid her head on that chest just days ago. Even now, the pull between them worked its way into her psyche, reminding her of his sexual appeal.

She chastised herself for being drawn to him. Then she swallowed and channeled her inner bitch. "Ethan, Nic, whoever you are. There's nothing to discuss. You played me. We fucked. You got caught lying. The end."

Ethan closed his eyes as he spoke. "That's not what this is, and you know it."

Gracie seized on his words. "No, Ethan. *I don't know it.* I don't know you. Until Friday, I didn't know your name. My God, Ethan. I shouted a fake name in the middle of an orgasm. How the hell do you think that makes me feel? How do you suppose we move beyond that?"

He opened his eyes and his gaze bored into hers. "It's not a fake name. My full name is Nicholas Ethan Hill. I stopped using Nicholas in professional circles a long time ago. Yes, you didn't know I was Ethan Hill, but you knew everything else. Everything I told you about my family, about my upbringing, about my hopes and dreams, all of that was true."

"Everything except your real name and the identity of the company you work for. The company that, had I not had my head so far up my ass, I would have asked to support LTN. Tell me this, was it your idea to work at LTN as Nicholas?"

"Yes."

"Why?" she asked.

"It was important to the board. I'd been in the press before, when I was at my previous company. I was trying to leave that part of my life behind."

"You're not a household name, Ethan."

"No, I'm not. But in the circles that matter to my company, I am. It's a small, competitive world that thrives on weaknesses within a company. I strive hard not to be a source of my company's weakness."

"So this is all about the company, to protect the company."

"Yes. No." He swiped a hand down his face. "I don't know."

"But you could have told me, right?"

"Yes."

"So either you didn't trust me or you didn't care enough about me to tell me who you are."

"That's not fair. Look at this from my perspective. Until Friday, we'd agreed to have a no-strings affair. We said there'd be no looking back after we went our separate ways."

"That's your excuse? That we wouldn't see each other again? Did it ever occur to you that years from now, as I looked back on this interlude, I would want to know the identity of the man who'd given me more than a dozen orgasms?"

"I was going to tell you."

He might as well have slapped her. *Did he think she was an idiot?* "Ethan, it doesn't matter what you *intended* to do. What matters is what you *did* do. And what you did do is lie to me for reasons that are, at worst, asinine, and at best, misguided. But in the end, you lied. And you compromised my ability to seek funding from Media Best. I gave you a task, Ethan. Give me a list of the companies who might be interested in LTN's work. Simple. But Media Best wasn't on the list you gave me, right? Now I know why. Not a good idea to ask your lover's company for money, don't you think?" She rubbed her temples. "God. Had I known your true identity, this relationship would not have happened."

When he closed his eyes again, Gracie's stomach twisted at the realization that he was well aware of that fact. She stumbled back, needing to distance herself from him. "Is that the real reason you didn't tell me who you are? You didn't want to compromise your ability to get in my bed? Or did you think I'd use you for the money? Become a gold digger you'd have to fend off?"

Ethan strode toward her and grabbed her arms, bringing her flush against him. "That's enough. Don't cheapen what we had together. Don't *do* this."

"We didn't have much together, Ethan. It was cheap the minute you became intimate with me knowing I didn't have a clue who you really were."

"Gracie—"

"Listen to me, Ethan. This is your issue, not mine. You need to figure out why you're so good at being something you're not. I really want that for you. But as for us, there is *nothing* you could say that would change the fact that we're over." She wrenched herself from his grasp and faced her window. "I'll be away on vacation for two weeks. If you care about me at all, you will use that time to complete as many service hours as you can. The assistant director in New York will be here and can certify your hours. With any luck, you can be done within a month. The sooner you're gone, the better."

"Gracie—"

She spun around. "Ethan, don't make this harder than it already is. If you could manage to think about someone other than yourself, just once, you'll do as I've asked."

They stared at each other, neither wanting to back down.

Finally, he spoke. "I'll go. But I'd like a chance to explain. Maybe someday you'll be ready to listen to me. I'll wait."

As she watched him leave her office, Gracie stifled the tears that begged to fall. He could wait all he wanted, but doing so would be a waste of his time.

CHAPTER EIGHTEEN

The occasional bang of pots and pans interrupted Gracie's fitful sleep. Why was she even trying to sleep? She wasn't going to get a decent night's rest for a long time.

She stared at the pale yellow ceiling above her childhood bed and wished she were anywhere but here. The bed provided no comfort, and the whimsical toys she'd played with as a child mocked her current mood. Most of all, her father's cheerful whistle, which accompanied his movements in the kitchen below, grated her. Her pain was her father's gain. Or so he thought.

She'd returned to Queens only two days ago. After a long talk with her mother, she'd shut herself in her old room, claiming she wasn't feeling well. Her mother now knew what had transpired between Gracie and Ethan. And Gracie had told her about LTN's troubles. Her mother, as usual, implored her to assess what had happened and figure out a way to move forward. That was the goal, of course. But it wouldn't be easy to achieve.

She was sure her mother had shared everything with her father. Gracie decided she couldn't avoid the inevitable conversation with her father, the one in which he told her that her ordeal was a sign that she should return home and take steps toward starting a family.

She lifted the comforter and slowly rose from the bed. After brushing her teeth and using the bathroom, she trudged down the stairs and joined her father in the kitchen.

Hector Ramirez shuffled around the kitchen in striped pajama bottoms and a Mets T-shirt. His dark brown hair, which still held its youthful luster, stood up in several directions. He wore glasses, which did nothing to improve his eyesight. He squinted as he read the side of a box of pancake mix.

Gracie sighed and sat down at the kitchen table. "Good morning."

He lowered his head and regarded her over the top of his glasses. "*Buenos dias*, Graciela. Would you like a cup of coffee? I just made some."

"Sure, *Papi*. That would be great." Despite her words, she'd failed to inject any enthusiasm into her voice.

Her father turned and searched for a coffee mug. Mug in hand, he poured her a cup of coffee and set it on the table. "I'm making pancakes."

"You?"

A playful grin spread across his face. "Yes, me. I can cook, you know."

That grin irked her. Really irked her. "That's a change. For the better, I mean."

Her father ignored her comment and measured the pancake

mix. Gracie, meanwhile, added cream and sugar to her coffee. "Go ahead, Dad. I know you want to talk about it."

He father stopped mixing the batter. "What do you think I want to talk about?"

"The reason I'm here. The reason I've been holed up in my old room."

Her father nodded, crossed the room, and joined her at the table. "Your mother told me what happened, yes. Graciela, I don't know what to think. This man. Is it serious?"

"I thought it was. But it turns out he was living a lie."

"A big strike against him. Has he explained why he lied?"

"He tried. But I wasn't really listening. And the excuse sounded like horseshit to me." Her father's ears turned red. "Sorry," she said.

He waved away her apology. "But you're still hurting."

Gracie nodded.

Her father sighed. "I don't know what to say. But I'll tell you this, *mija*. Your mother and I are here for you. You can come home anytime you want. You can stay with us. You don't have to go back to D.C. if you don't want to."

His hopeful expression tore her up inside. Gracie chewed on her lip to stem the venomous words at the edge of her lips. What emerged was a lukewarm version of what she really wanted to say to him. "You'd love that, wouldn't you? What is it that you want exactly? Do you want me to come home so I can spend the rest of my days taking care of you and *Mami*? Or do you want me to come home and search for a suitable husband who'll take care of me?"

Her father crossed his arms over his chest. "There's nothing wrong with a man taking care of his wife and family, Graciela. I did it."

Gracie's voice shook. "I *know* there's nothing wrong with a man taking care of his family. But there's nothing wrong with a woman taking care of herself, either. Women have choices, *Papi*. They can *choose* to work, or they can *choose* not to. But it's a choice. You've never approved of my choice to pursue a career. And now that my career is on shaky ground, you're happy. And that makes me incredibly sad. For you. For me. For Karen."

"Graciela—"

"No, *Papi*. I'll figure this out on my own. I don't expect you to understand."

* * *

Gracie's first week of vacation was almost over. In that week, she'd acquired a moping uniform, which consisted of black sweatpants, a white T-shirt, and a ratty sky blue robe that no longer resembled its former self. But the robe had pockets, an essential accessory for a woman who gorged on M&M's.

She slept, watched television, and reacquainted herself with at least a dozen different flavors of ice cream. Even she was annoyed by her glum mood. She couldn't seem to pull herself out of her self-induced funk, however.

She knew why. It gave her an excuse to hide from the responsibilities that awaited her in Washington. They wouldn't go away no matter how much she wished they would. And yes, she had no desire to revisit the moments she shared with Ethan.

He hadn't contacted her while she was away. Not that she'd

expected him to. Well. That wasn't entirely true. In fact, she had expected him to, and the fact that he hadn't only confirmed how little she'd meant to him.

When she'd begun to talk to the television, she knew she was in trouble. The notion that a man would turn her inside out and reduce her to this idiotic mess baffled her. *Who was this woman?* Even when she'd learned of Neal's betrayal, she'd bottled her disappointment and handled the aftermath with dignity. This was different. *She* was different. But she didn't want to think about the hows or the whys. The answers would only disappoint her.

Later that afternoon, when her father came home from work, he took one look at her as she lay on the couch and ordered her to shower.

Ignoring him, she snuggled into her blanket and reached for the remote. "I showered this morning."

Hector Ramirez's mouth gaped. "Let me get this straight. You showered this morning and *dressed* in that getup?"

"Sure did," she said.

He strode to the couch and grabbed the remote from her. "Graciela, this isn't you."

Gracie righted herself, wincing at the worn slippers that peeked under the blanket's edge. "Better?"

He said nothing, so she stared at him. Her father wore his regular electrician's uniform, a navy polo emblazoned with the company's logo and gray cargo pants. His electrician's license had put food on their table. And at Christmastime, their house was the brightest spot on the tree-lined block. He'd been her hero when she was young, but over the years, and after she'd left home in particular, their views had clashed in important ways.

After several ticks of silence, he ambled toward her and hit the side of her thigh, motioning for her to give him space on the couch. He sat down, twisting the baseball cap in his hands. Then he took a deep breath through his nose, causing his chest to rise and fall. "I'm going to tell you something, and I hope you don't get upset with me."

"Go on."

"We need you to leave."

Gracie's head snapped back. "Excuse me?"

"It's time for you to go home. To D.C. The Graciela I know doesn't mope about a job or a man. The Graciela I know would be in D.C. busting her butt trying to get money for her organization. The Graciela I know wouldn't stuff her face with junk food over a guy."

Gracie heard every word. He was right. But what did he have to gain by pointing out her sorry state? "This is what you want, isn't it?"

He sucked his teeth. A very bad habit of his. "No, Graciela. This isn't what I want for you at all."

"What *do* you want?"

"I want you to be the best damn director of LTN you can be. I want you to find love. I want grandchildren."

"That appears out of the question at the moment."

"I don't mean this minute. When you find the right man. Someone who will treasure you."

She'd never heard her father utter anything like this before. There had to be a catch. "What brought all this on?"

"Your mother."

"Mami?"

"Yes. I don't need to tell you how persuasive she can be with just a few words. Last night, she asked me what I wanted most for my daughters. And I didn't have to think about it. I told her I wanted you and Karen to be happy."

"And how does that change things?"

"Look at you, Graciela. You're not happy, and I have you right where I want you. With just a look, your mother made me realize that I was being selfish. You don't come home enough, but when you do, you're glowing, and you're excited about your job. Karen is, too. Excited about school, I mean. How can I deny my daughters that?"

"What led to this epiphany? Old age?"

"See there. That's the Graciela I know. Look, I'll be honest. I hate that you live so far away."

Gracie sighed. "D.C.'s a train ride away."

"That may be true. But when I grew up, the family stayed together. Aunts and uncles lived within minutes of each other. Cousins spent the night on weekends. You and your cousins went off to college, moved beyond the neighborhood. It's what we wanted for you, but I didn't realize it would mean I wouldn't get to see you. I expected my kids to live near me. I expected you'd drop off the grandbabies here so we could spoil them. I'm not going to pretend I love it, but I'm ready to accept it."

Her father's gaze fell to the floor in front of him. Gracie studied the lines on his forehead, noticed the crow's feet that pinched the skin around his eyes even when he wasn't smiling. He'd weathered a lot for his family over the years, reinventing himself and learning new skills as the changing economy demanded it.

He loved his family, and his resistance to change stemmed from his fear that he was losing his little girls.

Gracie moved closer to him and rested her head on his shoulder. "I love you."

"I love you too, *mija*."

"And you're never going to lose me. You'll always be a part of my life. And if I get married—"

"When you get married . . ."

Gracie wouldn't expect anything less of the mule. "*If* I get married, and if I'm lucky enough to have children, they'll know their grandfather. And I'll look the other way when you spoil them rotten. Deal?"

Her father turned and kissed her on the forehead. "Deal."

Gracie threw off the comforter and rose from the couch. "I'm going to buy a train ticket. I'll leave on Sunday."

Hector Ramirez stood and hugged her. "I can't believe I'm saying this, but I'm glad you're leaving."

Gracie smiled. Sure, he wasn't comfortable with the physical distance between them, but it was something he would have to get used to. She was committed to making Washington, D.C., her home.

Her father was right. She *could* have a career and a family; she didn't have to give up one to have the other. It wouldn't happen today. Not even tomorrow. But someday. Given the dismal state of her love life, though, someday was probably a long time from now.

CHAPTER NINETEEN

Ethan sat in his office chair and stared out the window. He'd pummeled the stress ball in his hands to no avail, so instead he simply tossed it up and caught it repeatedly.

A quick tap at his door elicited a growl low in his throat. "What?" he said.

Mark stuck his head through the door. The rest of him followed despite Ethan's best death stare.

Mark stood before him and grabbed the stress ball in midair. With his second best death stare of the day, Ethan reached into his desk drawer and withdrew another stress ball. He smiled at Mark and tossed the ball in the air.

"I've never argued with the fact that you have plenty of balls," Mark said.

Ethan grimaced. "What do you need, Mark?"

Mark set the stress ball on Ethan's desk and stuck his hands in his pockets. "Two things. One. The staff is running scared. Your assistant, for one, thinks you're going to blow her head off. And two, said assistant mentioned you're going on a trip. To Vegas."

"I'm not going to blow her head off, and Vegas is none of your business."

Mark sat down. "That's where you're wrong. Vegas is trouble. Trouble for you. And trouble for me, because I'll be the one to have to bring your sorry ass back from whatever gutter you find yourself in."

"I'm just going for the weekend. I need to get away."

"Ethan, are we going to pretend those three years didn't happen? The gambling? The booze? The women? What happens in Vegas is going to get your sorry ass fired."

"Stop being so fucking melodramatic. I'm going to decompress, that's all."

"I call bullshit. This is about that woman at the nonprofit. What happened?"

"Her name is Gracie and nothing happened."

"I call bullshit again. Vegas means you're trying to forget something. I'm done for the evening, so if you plan on heading to Vegas, I'll be going, too. You might as well tell me."

Ethan massaged his temples. "There's not much to tell. We had a thing. She found out who I was. She's pissed. We're done."

"Holy shit. You had *sex* with her?"

"Many, many times."

"And she didn't know your real name, or who you are?"

"Right."

"I should slap you on her behalf. What the fuck were you thinking?"

Ethan sprang from his chair and paced. "I wasn't thinking. I don't know what I thought. This was supposed to be a no-strings affair, so I didn't think it would matter."

"Even I know that's a load of crap. Wait. You didn't tell her that, did you?"

"I did."

"Jeez, Ethan. You're a dick *and* an idiot. Makes me wonder why you're regarded as such a prize."

"Fuck you, Mark. You were the one who suggested I complete my hours at that place."

Mark leaned back and raised his hands in the air. "Oh, no. Don't blame me for your screwup. I thought you'd get to know her. And if it ever got beyond the casual acquaintance stage, you'd tell her who you are. I never expected you to continue the farce after sleeping with her."

That's exactly what he should have done, but it hadn't worked out that way. His idiocy had gotten in the way. "I didn't know how to tell her. By the time things got heavy between us, she liked Nicholas Hill. *I liked Nicholas Hill.* I wanted to be that guy. An unassuming computer consultant with a life beyond these walls."

Mark cocked his head and regarded him. "You didn't want her to learn about your past."

Ethan frowned. "What?"

"You heard me. This is about your old position at Global Systems. And what went down afterward."

"You don't know what you're talking about."

"Maybe I don't. Maybe I do. But I know this. By heading to Vegas, you're trying to get away from something. This job. Your troubles with Gracie. Your past. I don't know. But you're running. And when you run, you get into trouble. And I'm the poor schmuck who ends up cleaning up your mess. I did it before, but I won't do it again."

"Mark, I'm okay. There's nothing to worry about."

Mark stared at him. Ethan glared back. They regarded each other like two men who'd just agreed to a gunfight at high noon.

Mark blinked first. "When you asked me to join you at Media Best, I jumped at the chance. Because I knew the man I'd work with at Global Systems was brilliant. Hotheaded but brilliant. Don't make an ass out of me. Let her see who you are, Ethan. You're not a criminal with a dark past, just a dipshit with an unflattering history. And don't make the same mistakes again. Fix it."

Ethan only nodded. Disparate thoughts collided in his brain, and he couldn't make sense of them all. Was Mark right? Had he kept up the ruse because he didn't trust her to like him despite his past? The possibility floored him.

Mark stretched his legs out in front of him. Then he rose from the chair. "Ethan, cancel the trip to Vegas. You don't need it. And ask yourself this. If you intended this to be a casual affair, why did you care so much about her opinion of you?"

Ethan had no answer.

Mark strode to the door. "The tech squad is upstairs discussing the Teleconnectiv launch. Maybe you should stick your head in."

Ethan's ears perked up. "What are they doing here this late?"

His friend shook his head in disbelief. "If you have to ask, then this job really has sucked the life out of you. It's pre-launch time, Ethan. Do you remember that excitement?"

When Ethan simply stared at him, Mark said, "No, I didn't think so." With a stiff salute and a shake of his head, Mark strolled out of his office.

Ethan threw the stress ball across the room. He needed a break.

* * *

The "break" led Ethan to the conference room on the top floor. There, he watched the engineers huddled around a long table. Empty pizza boxes littered the table, interspersed between laptops of various sizes. *Very expensive laptops.* He'd approved the expenditure himself.

When they saw him, the laidback air in the room froze, as though a billion feel-good atoms were suspended in air, ready to disintegrate the instant he opened his mouth. A few of his employees removed their feet from the table. Others straightened their workspaces, throwing the empty pizza boxes beside them on the floor. Ethan hated that they didn't feel comfortable around him. The suit created a wall between them, signifying that he signed checks, answered to the board, and strategized about the big picture. But the details? These men and women performed the company's technical work.

He left his place at the door and sat down among them. "Relax, ladies and gentlemen. I come in peace."

Gillam Bart, a young engineer who'd made himself indispensable to the team, spoke first. "Mr. Hill, the launch is on track. We're hashing out a few glitches, but they're nothing major."

Ethan removed his jacket and draped it over the back of his chair. "Tell me about the glitches. Walk me though it."

The software they'd designed had sprung from an idea he'd

pitched to the board years ago. He'd left his old firm disillusioned and disgraced. But his ideas remained part of his core, no matter how many bad personal decisions he'd made, and he'd used those ideas to convince Media Best he would excel as the company's CEO.

"Okay, the first has to do with connectivity. We've designed this video call service to be seamless. Whatever smartphone you have, it will work, right?"

Ethan nodded. "Right. We need to be able to deliver on that promise."

"But the lag for certain smartphones is greater than others, and nothing indicates the phone is the issue. It's something in the software."

Ethan rolled up his sleeves. "Could this be an issue with the network?"

"We don't think so. Here's why." Gillam jumped up from his chair and paced. "You sure you want us to walk you through everything?"

Ethan motioned for Gillam to continue. "Everything."

Hours later, Ethan rolled his shoulders and popped open a can of soda. "Great work, folks. There's more to be done, but you're on the right track. Now go home and get some rest. This work will be waiting for you on Monday."

A collective groan suggested they didn't appreciate the reminder, but Ethan knew better. He'd watched and listened. And what he saw inspired him to rethink his career path. His life path, really. These men and women enjoyed their jobs. Hashing out new ideas or resolving problems excited them. It excited him, too. But as CEO, he no longer brainstormed. That was someone else's job. And the resulting frustration had nearly driven him to repeat the mistakes of his past.

No more. This time, rather than engage in destructive behavior to diffuse his frustration, he was going to change his situation altogether. Sure, he wanted to make the most of the opportunities he'd been afforded, but he wouldn't do so at the expense of his own happiness.

As for what he would do about Gracie? Ethan had no clue.

CHAPTER TWENTY

Gracie returned to her apartment the weekend before she was due back at the office. When she reached the second-floor landing, she spotted an unmarked manila envelope propped against her door.

She carried her bags into her apartment, placed the envelope on the coffee table, and dropped onto her couch. The train ride had exhausted her, but this time she hadn't suffered through it with a talkative college student by her side. The relative quiet had given her several hours to plan her next steps. The ideas she'd come up with, which she'd jotted on a napkin, gave her new hope for LTN's future. She wouldn't give up. She would push through her heartbreak and focus her energy on saving LTN's Washington, D.C., facility.

Heartbreak.

She'd never experienced it. Until now. Yes, she'd been hurt by her ex-boyfriend's betrayal, but she'd placed Neal firmly in her past and vowed to learn from that particular mistake.

Almost two weeks after learning Ethan's identity, she still moved within a bubble of sadness that belied her attempts to keep his memory at arm's length. Even now she pictured the images of their lovemaking on this couch, of the way he'd shouted her name in unbridled pleasure. The mental replay elicited a frustrated groan. *Enough*, she told herself. It was time to move on.

Gracie sat up and reached for the manila envelope. Unable to contain her curiosity, she ripped it open and peeked inside. Someone had stuffed newspaper clippings and sheets of paper inside. Turning the envelope upside down, she watched its contents scatter on the coffee table. Her heart leaped when she saw Ethan's stationery—and she grimaced when she remembered the last time he'd sent her a note, the time he'd sent her cash to repay her for the birthday gift she'd tried to give him.

The knowledge that Ethan had sent the envelope dampened her curiosity. She shot up from the couch and headed to the kitchen for a cup of coffee. Minutes later, as she sipped a steaming cup of java, she eyed the pile of papers on the coffee table. What was that hackneyed phrase? Curiosity killed the cat? Well, me-fucking-ow. She couldn't resist.

Gracie strode across the room and settled herself on the couch. Then she spread the papers on the coffee table, lifting Ethan's note to her nose, searching for his signature scent. Nothing.

The words summoned her tears: *After you've had a chance to review this, call me. Please. I need to explain. Yours, Ethan.*

She sniffed and wiped her eyes. His bold writing reminded her of his strong hands, his long fingers, the veins that traveled from his knuckles to his muscled forearms. Her mind wandered, clamoring to return to the days when his warm breath puffed against her ear, when his early morning stubble scraped against her skin, when his cock stretched her. *Good Lord, she was in trouble.*

She stared at the papers, a few of which included photographs of Ethan, not knowing where to begin. She moved the papers around, noting a few were screenshots of social media pages. Order. They needed to be placed in chronological order. After accomplishing that task, Gracie began to read.

The first news item was a small announcement in a local paper, *The Hanover Reporter*. It congratulated Ethan on his acceptance to the University of Pennsylvania on a four-year scholarship. It noted that his parents, lifelong residents of the town and employees of a local food plant, were thrilled their son had been given the opportunity.

The second news item, published six years later in that same paper, announced Ethan's graduation from business school.

Years later, the New York dailies reported Ethan's engagement to Bella Sedrick, a New York socialite-in-training whose father chaired the board of Global Systems, a technology company. The news blurb ended with a snarky comment questioning whether the company had created Ethan's new position as a reward for his promise to marry Bella.

After that, a flurry of news blurbs chronicled Ethan's rise within the company and his membership in an elite circle of young professionals with pedigreed backgrounds. Lots of partying, lots of drinking, and very public arguments with Bella about his behavior followed. The gossip columns reported Ethan's supposed infidelity, gambling bouts, and drunken behavior. And if the pictures of his swinging fists were any indication, Ethan gave the gossip rags plenty to write about.

The second to last news blurb reported Ethan's arrest—for solicitation—and his quick release from jail. The last item announced in a two-sentence blurb that Bella had ended their engagement.

Gracie sat back and dropped her head against the sofa.

The man reflected in the reports bore no resemblance to the man she knew. And yet. If she'd known his past, would she have given him a chance? Probably not. And what of his erratic and irresponsible behavior? What had caused it? Was that what he wanted to explain?

She picked up her phone and called him. He picked up after the first ring, as though he'd been waiting for her call.

"Gracie," he whispered.

His voice wrapped around her like velvet. It would be so easy to forgive him, but her heart admonished her to be cautious. "I'm ready to listen," she said.

"When?"

"Now if you'd like. I'm back from New York."

"I'll be there in ten minutes." He hung up before she could suggest a neutral meeting place. But if they met in public, she might cry, might engage in histrionics. She cringed at that possibility.

He buzzed her apartment nine minutes after he'd disconnected their call. Her heart tripped at the sight of him. His disheveled appearance did nothing to diminish the ache in her chest or the urge to circle her arms around him. His eyes lacked the brilliance she'd come to expect, and the shadow of stubble across his cheeks indicated he'd skipped his usual grooming habits. The stubborn part of her took comfort in his obvious distress. The rational part of her mentally scolded herself for being so childish.

He stood at the threshold of her apartment. "Hi. Thanks for seeing me."

"To be honest, I feel like an ass for listening. But I read the papers you sent me. I know you would have preferred for that to be a part of your past, so I can give you this. Come in."

Ethan unzipped his jacket and walked inside. "May I?" he asked as he pointed to the couch.

Gracie wrapped her oversized cardigan around her waist and folded her arms over her chest. "Yes." She sat in the recliner across from him, not trusting herself to be near him.

"I'll explain in a minute, but I want to start with this. I'm sorry. I'm sorry I lied to you. I'm sorry I didn't trust you. I'm sorry you found out about me in the way that you did. I'm so fucking sorry. About everything. Whatever else happens between us, you need to know that I never meant to hurt you."

Gracie's brain scrambled for something sarcastic to say, but the words wouldn't come. His eyes, tired and lifeless, pleaded for her understanding. She'd never seen him this way, unsure and struggling to make his point. Still, she didn't want to bend to him, not after what he'd done, and she desperately needed a barrier to protect herself against the sincerity in his voice. "Is there an explanation forthcoming?"

Ethan pressed his lips together and nodded. "I grew up in a rural area outside Harrisburg. My parents didn't have much, but they loved my sister and me. For years, I watched my parents come home from their shift work. Exhausted. Troubled about finances. They never complained. But I knew it was hard on them.

I vowed to help them. Decided I'd take any opportunity to give them a better life."

Ethan stretched out his legs and stared at his shoes.

"I read about your engagement. When did you meet Bella?" Gracie asked.

Ethan lifted his chin and clenched his jaw. "I met Bella after I'd graduated from business school. She was my first serious girl-friend. She wasn't a breath of fresh air, she was a hurricane. She stormed into my life, and I was so flattered that a girl with her up-bringing and connections was interested in me, I got caught up in her, in her world. Before I knew it, her father had become my mentor and had promised me a place in his company."

"What went wrong?"

"I wasn't happy. Not with Bella. And not with my job. It was great in the beginning, when I was doing what I loved. But as I moved up the ranks, my love for the job waned. As did my desire to be with Bella and adapt to her lifestyle."

"Judging by the pictures, you seemed to take to it very well."

"I acted like a jackass, all in an effort to numb myself. I didn't know what I was doing, alienated my family the few times I came back to visit. Missed my niece's birth because I had box seats for an NFL game, courtesy of Bella's dad. I gambled. Drank too much. I was a fucking mess. Bella was the darling of New York's high society scene. I was the working-class upstart riding on her gravy train. Or that's how the gossip mongers painted me."

"And the arrest? For solicitation, I mean. What the hell was that about?"

"Gracie, I swear it was a setup."

Gracie stared at him and raised her eyebrows.

"I'm not lying. I got trashed in a hotel bar. A gorgeous woman sidled up to me. Thirty minutes later, I was in the back of a squad car. The woman confessed to the cops that she'd been paid to do it. They didn't even bring charges. But a tenacious reporter for a gossip rag had been tipped about the incident and was there to take my photograph as I left the police precinct."

"Who would do something like that to you?"

"Bella. Her father. Who knows? They never admitted it. Bella wasn't an angel. Our fights had just as much to do with her infidelities as my gambling and drinking. I suspected the whole setup was their way of making Bella look like the victim. But when I confronted Papa Bear about it, he scoffed at the idea that he'd be involved. Seconds later, though, he offered to put in a good word for me at Media Best. Said Bella would break the engagement and we'd move on. Quietly."

"And being the CEO at another tech company wasn't what you wanted, right?"

Ethan figured Gracie would understand. She'd picked up on his dissatisfaction with his career almost from the outset of their relationship. "You're right. I didn't want the position at Media Best. But when I went home with my tail between my legs, the disappointment on my parents' faces rocked me. All their lives, they'd struggled. And what had I done? I'd made an ass of myself. The position at Media Best was a way for me to show them that I wasn't tarnished goods. That I hadn't wasted the opportunities I'd been given."

"Is that what they wanted for you?" she asked.

"They want me to be happy. But I ran so fast and so far away from my former life that I didn't think about what would make me happy. I just went with it, and then I continued to resent the demands of my position."

"Okay. It's all coming together in my head now. And your stint at LTN allowed you to escape your past. To engage with people who didn't know anything about your background. And that's why you never told me who you were."

"Right."

Everything he'd told her swirled in her head. When she placed Ethan's deceit in the context of his past, she understood its impetus. She couldn't absolve him for what he'd done, but she understood now that his decision to withhold his identity stemmed from his embarrassment. What a mess. But it was his mess, not hers. "Thanks for the explanation," she said as she stood. "I didn't realize how much I needed this. Closure, I guess."

Ethan looked up at her and scrunched his face. "Closure?"

Gracie steeled herself. "Yes, closure. Ethan, I appreciate the explanation, but that's all it was. It doesn't change the fact that you're not the man I thought you were. It doesn't change the fact that you lied to me. That you started a relationship with me, knowing that you weren't being truthful about yourself."

He stood and paced. "Gracie, I understand why you're angry, but I shared this with you because I want you to know everything, because I want to share a future with you. I told you everything that mattered."

Her heart tempted her to forgive him, but her pride rejected the idea out of hand. "You don't get to decide what matters, Ethan. A relationship means you share the important parts of yourself."

He strode to her and placed his hands on her upper arms. "But that's just it, Gracie. I did share the important parts of myself. My professional goals, my fears, stuff about my family. You can't discount that so easily."

Yes, she could. Everything about their relationship made her doubt herself. She'd lost herself in him. Hadn't picked up on the signs that something was amiss. She should have questioned him more about his work, about his past.

When she failed to respond, he pulled her to him and wrapped his arms around her. Gracie stood motionless, sapped of any energy to do more than that. Ethan's chin pressed against her ear. "Gracie, listen to me. I want to start over. No bullshit about casual affairs. No limitations. We commit to each other."

His words gutted her. He didn't understand, and she suspected he never would. He viewed his willingness to commit to her as a prize for which she should be grateful, as though it alone would absolve him of what he'd done. In short, he was this year's version of Neal, which gave her an idea, a way to ensure he'd leave her alone.

Infusing her voice with feigned confidence, she said, "I can't make that leap. Given what's happened between us, it's not a risk I'm willing to take. I'm willing to return to our arrangement, however."

Ethan stepped back and his jaw went slack. "Until my hours are completed?"

"Yes. This time we'd go into it without any pretenses. No lies, no promises of a future. Just enjoying each other for what it is."

"That's all you're prepared to give me?"

"Yes."

Ethan scrubbed his hands down his face. "I can't fault you for putting up walls. I screwed up. But what you're proposing isn't enough. We're well beyond that."

"I disagree. And that's all I'm prepared to give."

His face hardened under her watchful gaze, but she pushed ahead, knowing he wouldn't agree to what she'd proposed. That was the point, after all.

"So I guess we're done here?" she asked.

Ethan grimaced and shoved his fingers through his hair. "Yeah. I guess we are. But if you change your mind, you know where to find me. Take care."

When the door clicked shut, Gracie dropped to the couch. She'd made the right choice. Still, she hadn't expected it to hurt so much.

CHAPTER TWENTY-ONE

The next morning, Gracie strode into the office prepared to do battle. LTN would not close its doors on her watch. Not until she'd explored every avenue and harassed every potential donor into considering LTN's cause.

Seconds after dropping into her chair and placing her purse in her desk drawer, her intercom buzzed. "Yes, Brenda?"

"Gracie, there's a gentleman from Digitech Corporation on line one. Harry Seville. Says he'd like to speak to you about LTN. Are you available?"

Gracie stopped straightening the papers on her desk and stared at the phone. She'd sent Digitech information about LTN weeks ago, thanks to Ethan's thorough list. "Sure, Brenda. I'll take the call."

When the line buzzed, Gracie snatched the phone from its cradle. "This is Graciela Ramirez."

"Ms. Ramirez, this is Harry Seville. I tried to reach you last week, but I understand you were on vacation. In any event, thank you for sending me information about LTN. I'm impressed by the operation."

Gracie's heart hammered in her chest. "Thank you, Mr. Seville."

"I must confess that while I'd intended to call you, I'd set your request at the end of the many requests we receive, particularly at year's end. But Media Best's former CEO convinced me to take a second look."

Gracie's head pounded. None of this made sense. Former CEO of Media Best? Surely, Mr. Seville was confused. "Did you say *former* CEO of Media Best?"

"Yes. Ethan Hill. He resigned last week. But before he did, he asked me to consider contributing to LTN's coffers. He gave an impassioned speech on LTN's behalf, explained that he'd seen the organization's good work firsthand after being sentenced to perform community service there."

"He told you all that?"

"He did. Anyway, I can't promise that we'd be able to make a substantial donation this fiscal year, but I'd love to meet with you and discuss ways Digitech can help LTN."

Gracie wanted to dance around her office. Instead, she simply replied, "Yes, yes. I'd love that, too. I have quite a few ideas about ways companies like yours could help, including a consortium of companies that would rotate financial contributions and volunteer services to LTN."

"Well, anything that would help us share the load with other companies has my attention. I'll have my assistant send you potential dates."

Gracie nodded her head even though Mr. Seville couldn't see her. "Sure, sure. I look forward to meeting with you soon. Thanks so much for the call."

Two similar calls followed in quick succession. Both callers, executives at area tech companies, remarked that Ethan had praised LTN's mission. Ethan had made those calls before he knew how she'd react to his explanation and apology. Gracie didn't know what to make of that fact.

A quick tap at her door startled her out of her catatonic state. Jason, one of her favorite clients, stood outside the door shifting back and forth.

"Hi, Jason," she said as she waved him inside. "Please sit."

"Hi, Ms. Martinez. I, uh, I wanted to thank you, for LTN . . . and everything."

"You're welcome, Jason. But what's this about? You sound like you're saying good-bye."

Jason pulled on the front of his jeans and shifted in his seat. "Well, I am. Sort of. I got a computer. It's all state of the art and everything. Courtesy of Mr. Hill. Ethan, I mean. So I'm not going to need a computer here anymore. I'll come to visit, but it won't be for the computers."

Gracie stared at him as she processed his words. "Mr. Hill gave you a computer?"

"His company did, yeah," Jason said. Then he stared at her with a quizzical expression. "Is everything all right?"

"How did you know his name was Ethan?"

Jason's shy smile transformed into a wide grin. "He told me. Said he didn't want to make a big fuss about who he is. Now that he's done, he said he wanted me to know." Jason shook his head from side to side and slouched farther into the chair. "I was dealing with a baller, and I didn't even know it."

"Baller?" Gracie asked.

"Yeah, you know. A baller. Shot caller. Head honcho. Never treated me like I was beneath him. I thought that was cool. Anyway, he said he thinks I have promise and wanted to be sure I had a computer for school."

"That was very nice of him."

"Yeah. So I'll see you around." Jason rose from his chair.

"Wait a minute, Jason. You're not getting off that easy."

Jason sank into the chair again. "What is it?"

"Mr. Hill's right that you have promise. I'd be a fool to let you walk out of here. Would you be interested in part-time work here?"

"What do you mean?"

"I've been thinking about a formal after-school program where kids would be exposed to programming, to tie into STEM classes at school. We'd need help. Nothing fancy. The basics of programming. My plan is to convince area programmers to train our most promising high school students. Then you guys would teach the kids, mostly primary school students. Interested?"

"And I'd be paid?"

Gracie knew most teenagers listened more closely when money was involved. "It's my hope that you'd be paid. And that the position might lead to an internship at a company in the area."

"I'm in."

"It's not solid yet, but I'll be in touch soon, okay?"

"Yeah. And thanks for everything."

They stood at the same time and shook hands. "This isn't good-bye," Gracie told him.

He nodded and walked out. Gracie walked to her office window and stared at the rain pelting against the pane. In a matter of hours, the tenor of her day had changed dramatically. And she'd been bombarded with so much information she wasn't sure she could process it.

What had prompted Ethan to resign from his position? Where was he now? In that moment, Jason's announcement that Ethan had completed his service hours sank in. Maybe she'd never see him again. That is, unless she reached out to him.

She walked out of her office and approached Brenda. "Mr. Hill completed his service hours while I was gone?"

Brenda looked away from her computer screen. "Yes. Debra signed off on his hours. He worked like a man possessed. Was here almost as much as I was."

Distracted by this information, Gracie trudged back to her desk. Of course, he deserved her gratitude. But did he deserve her forgiveness? Could she look past his deceit and accept his apology?

After searching for a contact number on her computer, Gracie dialed Media Best's number and asked to speak with Mark Lansing.

"This is Mark."

"Mr. Lansing, you might not remember me—"

"Graciela Ramirez, right?"

How odd that he remembered her and recalled the sound of her voice. "Yes, that's right. I'm looking for Ethan. Do you know where I might find him?"

"Yeah. He went to visit his family in Pennsylvania. He'll be back in the office on Wednesday."

"Oh, I thought he resigned?"

"He did. From his position as CEO. He's now head of software development. Plans to work in the office two days a week. Otherwise, he'll be working from home. We couldn't refuse him, and as the new CEO, I wasn't prepared to let him go."

"Congratulations," Graciela said.

"I think the right phrase might be 'good luck,'" Mark said. "I have incredibly competent shoes to fill."

"Right. Good-bye." Gracie placed the receiver back in its cradle.

She wouldn't be able to talk to him for two days. Could she wait that long? She guessed she would have to, because what she wanted to say to him could only be said in person. For now, though, she had to prepare for her meeting with Belinda Cantrell of the Blakely Foundation, her only viable source for a quick and sizable influx of cash. If it went well, LTN would have enough funding for another fiscal year. If it didn't go well, Gracie might soon be out of a job.

* * *

"Ms. Ramirez," the receptionist said. "Ms. Cantrell will see you now."

Gracie smoothed her skirt and gave herself a mental pep talk. *You can do this. Show her you believe in LTN's mission. Show her you're worthy of her confidence.* With a deep breath, Gracie followed the receptionist to Ms. Cantrell's office.

Clad in a wool red suit, Ms. Cantrell sat at a large desk that dwarfed her diminutive figure. When Gracie strode across the large office, Belinda Cantrell smoothed her brilliant white hair, which surrounded her head like a cloud. Ms. Cantrell's elegant appearance warred with the raspy voice Gracie had heard over the phone. "Ms. Ramirez, it's a pleasure to meet you in person. Please sit."

"The pleasure is mine, Ms. Cantrell," Gracie said.

"I'd like to keep this brief. I've read the materials you sent. Tell me how the city's residents benefit from LTN?"

Gracie swallowed and perched on her chair. "As I'm sure you're aware, the Internet has revolutionized the way Americans conduct business. People apply for jobs online, people complete business transactions online, the Internet opens up a world of resources for research and learning. But what of residents who don't have regular access to computers, poor students in particular? The continuing problem of the learning gap between such students and students with more resources is compounded by the Internet."

Gracie ventured a glance at Ms. Cantrell. Was she even listening?

"Please continue, Ms. Ramirez."

* * *

Gracie had done the best that she could. She hoped it was enough.

"Very impressive, Ms. Ramirez. Before we go any further, I wanted to ask you about your connection to Ethan Hill."

Gracie's heart pounded in her chest. "I'm sorry?"

"Ethan Hill. You know him, yes?"

"I do. But what does that have to do with LTN?"

"Well, as you might imagine, Ms. Ramirez, the Bentley Foundation would like to partner with organizations that are above reproach. Mr. Hill is a wild card, wouldn't you say? "

Gracie couldn't believe what she was hearing. Why was this woman asking about Ethan, and why did it matter? "Ms. Cantrell, Ethan Hill is no longer associated with LTN. But for the record, the man I know is honorable and nothing like the man the media portrayed him to be. He was the subject of bad press years ago. What he did then has no bearing on the man he is now."

"That may be, but those are the kinds of questions the trustees will ask."

"Why? Why would they care about Mr. Hill?"

"Because Mr. Hill took out an ad in today's *Post* in which he encouraged his corporate colleagues to find ways to expand Internet access to the city's lower-income residents. You haven't seen it?"

"No, I haven't."

"He wrote that he'd spent time at LTN as a result of a community service sentence, which makes me think Mr. Hill hasn't gotten his reckless ways out of his system."

"He admitted *that* in the *Post*?"

Gracie didn't know what to think. Ethan had disclosed to the city the very information the company's board wanted to keep quiet. Why?

"Yes, he did. In any event, I need to know that Mr. Hill's

connection to LTN won't be a distraction that will make others question the foundation's decision to support your organization."

Gracie clamped down on her bottom lip. The nerve of this woman. Who was she to treat Ethan like damaged goods? "Ms. Cantrell, forgive me for saying so, but Mr. Hill's personal history is none of the foundation's business. If Mr. Hill matters at all, the man he is today should dispense with any of your concerns."

She'd find a way to save LTN, with or without the foundation's help, and she wouldn't turn her back on Ethan to do it. "Ms. Cantrell, if my connection to Mr. Hill is problematic, I'll seek help elsewhere." Gracie rose and straightened her suit jacket. "I'm sorry to have wasted your time."

"Ms. Ramirez, relax. Let me finish, please."

Against her better judgment, Gracie returned to her seat.

Ms. Cantrell's face softened. "We have a friend in common."

Gracie struggled to keep the surprise out of her voice. "We do?"

"Yes. Ethan Hill."

Gracie peered at Ms. Cantrell, noticing only then the humor in the woman's eyes. "How do you know Ethan?"

"We met a few years ago at a charity event. I took a liking to him instantly. Easy on the eyes, wouldn't you say?"

It was official. Gracie had been transported to an alternate universe. "Yes."

"I spoke with him this morning, after seeing today's ad in the paper. I imagine Ethan expected I'd see it. He's a methodical man, and I'm a nosy old coot. I asked him why he didn't arrange for Media Best to make a donation. Can you guess what he said?"

Gracie shook her head in the negative.

Ms. Cantrell smiled. "He said you'd turn it down. And he said he wasn't meant to be your knight in shining armor anyway."

The ice around Gracie's heart melted when she realized the implication of Ms. Cantrell's words. He'd understood how important it was for her to rescue LTN on her own terms. Understood, too, that although she wouldn't turn down a good word based on LTN's merits, she didn't want a handout, either, particularly given their previous sexual relationship. All those times they'd discussed her professional goals, he'd listened.

"For the record, your application for support was approved a week ago, *before I knew about your connection to Ethan.* Today's interview was a formality," Ms. Cantrell said. With a sheepish smile, she explained, "More than anything, I'm a sucker for a good love story."

Gracie's heart pounded. Love. That's exactly what it was. Distilled to its essence, what Gracie felt for Ethan was love. And he loved her, too. The lengths to which he'd gone to help LTN at the expense of his privacy certainly showed that. Gracie stood, causing her purse to drop to the floor. "Thank you so much, but I have to go." She rushed to pick up her purse and a few of its contents that had scattered on the floor.

"Yes, I imagine you have unfinished business with Mr. Hill."

Gracie smiled as she rose, and then she shook Ms. Cantrell's hand. "Thank you. Thank you so much."

Before Gracie flew through the door, Ms. Cantrell stopped her. "Ms. Ramirez, one more thing."

"Yes?"

"You might be his."

"His?"

"*His* knight in shining armor. Given what he wrote in the paper, that's the conclusion I came to. Not that my opinion matters, of course."

Gracie knew differently. Ethan didn't need to be saved. He just needed someone who would stand by him. For a lifetime.

Could she be that person? She'd sure as hell try. But to succeed, she'd need help.

CHAPTER TWENTY-TWO

Ethan stared at his computer screen, but the numbers and symbols made no sense to him. His brain refused to focus on the task at hand.

For years, he'd assumed his restless spirit masked his disenchantment with the state of his career. Not enough success. Too much success. But now that he'd secured the right place for himself within the company, dissatisfaction still coursed through him.

He wanted to commit to something he loved and do it well. And as usual, his thoughts strayed to Gracie. He wanted to love *her* and do it well. But Gracie refused to forgive him, and he couldn't blame her. Maybe he'd been too hasty in rejecting her offer of a casual affair. Maybe it was better to have some of Gracie than none. But he dismissed that thought as quickly as it had come to him. He knew himself. He didn't deal in half measures. He wanted her to be his woman. *Only his.*

Mark rushed through his door and slammed it behind him. "Take the job back, please."

Ethan laughed, taking in Mark's harried expression and his mussed hair. "Job's got you pulling your hair out already?"

Mark paced his office. "You should have warned me. And why the hell are you on a different floor? I'm going to need your advice, man. Twenty times a day, if not more. You should be on the tenth floor with me."

Ethan stretched. Mark required handling. *A lot of handling.* "You'll be fine. And I'm here. What's going on?"

Mark hit the back of his head on Ethan's door. "Sign this. Decide this. Go to this. Crap. I had no idea you did so much shit while I was crunching numbers."

"You'll get used to it. This position was made for you."

"You owe me."

"I do?"

"Yeah. Imagine if I'd turned down the position. You would have had to remain CEO while we searched on the outside."

Ethan's bullshit detector emitted a quick succession of pings. Not true at all. If he hadn't stepped down before placing that ad in the *Post,* the board would have made the decision for him. Still, Mark was angling for a favor, and Ethan chose to play along. "What do you need?"

"I need to go to Happy Hour. Join me."

It was the last thing Ethan wanted to do, but Mark had always been there for him. Joining him for a quick beer at the bar on the corner was the least Ethan could do. "Sure, I'll meet you in the lobby in ten minutes."

* * *

Ethan and Mark sat at the bar of Citizen Jane, a favorite among the executives and lawyers who worked near Connecticut Avenue.

Ethan faced the bar and nursed a beer. Mark faced the room, whiskey in hand.

The dark colors and hazy lighting matched Ethan's mood. But the place was too noisy, filled with people who didn't seem to have a care in the world. Ethan envied them.

Ethan glanced at Mark, who dodged and ducked in an effort to spot any newcomers who entered through the bar's revolving door. "Looking for someone, Mark?"

Mark spun around. "No. I'm good. Just tired."

Ethan dropped his head. "I know the feeling. It'll get better. You have a team that wants you to succeed, myself included."

Mark didn't respond.

What was the point of this whole outing? Ethan took a swig of his beer and placed the bottle on the counter. He dug in his pocket for his wallet so he could tip the bartender.

"I'm going to head home," he said, wincing at the bar's garish décor. As a nod to the season, the establishment had strewn tacky tinsel and paper icicles everywhere. The haphazard holiday decorations mocked him at every turn. Merry Christmas, and a Bah Humbug to you, too.

How was he going to get through the holiday season? Without Gracie. Ethan took a deep breath and the scent of lilacs wafted over him. He whipped his head up, and his heart banged against his chest. *Gracie.* There she sat, on the stool that Mark had occupied, looking edible in a tight black skirt with a slit up its front. Her crossed legs flashed patches of her luscious thighs.

"Hi," she said with a half smile.

Ethan struggled to assemble a coherent thought. He forced his lips to move. "Hi."

"My name's Graciela Ramirez. What's yours?"

"Nicholas Ethan Hill. But I go by Ethan."

"It's nice to meet you, Ethan. Do you work around here?"

He dropped back, taking in her relaxed posture and the waves of hair that framed her face. God, he hoped this meant she was willing to give him a second chance. "Yeah, I work around the corner."

"Doing what?" she asked.

"Head of software development."

"Sounds important."

He shrugged. "It pays the bills. I'm busy, but I have time to get home to cook dinner."

"You like cooking, do you?"

His eyes bored into hers, willing her to understand the implication of his words. "I'm not much of a cook, but I'm willing to learn."

Her smile widened. "I'm new in town. Transferred from New York. I run a community service organization just off Columbia Road."

"Do you plan to stay in the city?" he asked.

"I do. I could use some help getting my bearings, though. D.C. is a difficult city to navigate. Would you be willing to help me?"

"I'd do anything for you."

Her nonchalance slipped, and she bit her lip. When she leaned into him, Ethan fought the instinct to grab her hand and shuttle her through the crowd. He needed her. Now. But he would follow her lead. This time, he'd do it her way, or not at all. Luckily for him, the urgency in her voice matched the urgency of his thoughts.

"Are you willing to take me home?" she asked.

"I'm not that kind of guy, but I'd make an exception for you."

Gracie laughed. "Here's a different question." She hesitated. He waited, tortured by the uncertainty of their future. She raised her shoulders and exhaled. "Are you willing to love me?"

Ethan's heart thumped in his chest. Relief flooded through him, like a blast of cold air against his skin on a sweltering day. It was the easiest question he'd had to answer in his thirty-two years. "I already do. Question is, can you do the same?"

She reached over and traced her fingers across his jaw. His body responded to the intimacy of her touch, knowing exactly whose fingers pressed against his face. In that moment, everyone at the bar disappeared. He turned his head and kissed her fingers. Her brown eyes fluttered closed. After several seconds, she opened them, gifting him with a clear and steady gaze. "I'm sure I can."

Ethan couldn't bear to continue this conversation in a crowded bar. "Let me take you home. We'll talk."

She rose as he did. "We'll talk tomorrow. Tonight, let's get reacquainted."

Ethan dropped his forehead to hers. Images of what they'd do to each other nearly propelled him to drop to his knees in the middle of the bar. He needed to get her home.

But first he needed reinforcements. "We'll have to stop at the store on the way to my place."

She hurried by his side as they made their way to the revolving door. "What do you need?"

He pressed his body close to hers as they circled out the door. "Coffee. Lots of coffee. And condoms. Lots of condoms."

She raised her hand to hail a cab. "Spending the weekend in bed, are we?"

"Yeah. In bed. On the couch. On the floor. In the shower. On the kitchen counter. You get the picture."

When the cab stopped at the curb, she opened the door and shoved him in. "We'll need whipped cream, too."

* * *

Ethan stored the canister of whipped cream in his fridge and turned to Gracie. "Think one canister's enough?"

She smiled and grabbed his hands, pulling him in the direction of his bedroom. "No worries. I'm sure we'll have plenty of cream tonight."

He stilled and burst out laughing. What the hell had gotten into her? "Did you just . . . Was that a cum joke, Gracie?"

She turned around and stuck out her tongue. "Ewww. You're right. Sometimes I have no filter."

They reached his bedroom door, the perfect place to make his point. "I don't want you to have a filter. Not with me. Not here. Not anywhere."

"I like the idea of that. You'll be the only one to know how dirty my thoughts can get."

Gracie. In his bedroom. With dirty thoughts. Have mercy on him, indeed.

She entered his room and fell back against the bed. He joined her within seconds, and once their bodies connected, their movements matched the pace of a thrill ride. Fast breaths. Heated skin. Frantic hands.

As for his hands, they traveled everywhere, bunching her clothes to reveal the supple skin underneath. Not long after, she sat up and without pretense or coyness discarded her blouse and bra. If she intended to break him, he predicted tonight she would meet her goal.

When he reached out to toy with her nipples, she fell back against the mattress, giving him freedom to roam. He caressed her nipples, alternating between featherlight touches and gentle pressure. In response, she lifted one thigh and dug her toes into the mattress, the arch of her foot revealing the tension she desperately needed to release. He took that as his cue to slip his hands between her legs. His intentions clear, she dropped her other thigh against the mattress, opening herself to him.

After readjusting himself to free his hands, he slid a finger under her thong and moved the fabric back and forth against her clit. She let out a soft moan, the sound causing his dick to stiffen as though it were responding to her command.

Gracie raised her torso and placed her elbows on the bed. Her glazed expression nearly undid him. She wanted to see what he was doing to her, and that was so fucking sexy to him.

When she bit her lip, looking too composed for his liking, he slipped a finger inside her and massaged her slick walls.

Her head fell back on a long groan. "Oh, God. Yes. Keep doing that."

He wanted her shaking with need, but she wasn't quite there. He moved down the bed, pressed a kiss against her inner thigh, and tapped his finger against her center. "Can I lick you there?"

She released a breathy moan before she answered. "For future reference, that kind of question is totally unnecessary."

Her smile, genuine and open, did exactly what it had always done to him: make him greedy for more. He wanted her happy, because she'd done the same for him. "I'll make a note of that." He rose to his knees. "Lift up."

She dug the toes of her feet into the mattress and raised her butt. He removed her skirt and thong with a few quick tugs and settled between her legs. "Are you wet enough for me, baby?"

"Not sure. Why don't you investigate?"

He waggled his eyebrows as he lifted her legs over his shoulders. "Roger that. I'm going in."

Her legs shook, likely from laughter, but his attention was drawn to the apex of her thighs. He pressed tender kisses against her mound as he stroked her flat belly, and her stomach quivered under his touch.

"Gracie, you're so pretty here. Wet and swollen, and it's driving me insane." He wasn't exaggerating. His cock tingled in anticipation of entering that slick heat, so much so that he rubbed his cock against the mattress to mimic what he'd soon be doing to her. He couldn't be bothered to be embarrassed by it, not when the magnificent woman on his bed was the catalyst.

She threaded her hands through the hair at the nape of his neck and pushed her mound closer to his mouth. "Ethan, please."

Fuck. This was what he wanted. What he needed to see. Gracie beside herself with want.

He took a long lick up her slit and fastened his mouth on her swollen clit. She jerked and cried out at the initial contact, but her moans quieted as she undulated her hips in a rhythm to match his flicks of her clit. The nub swelled against his tongue, and he moaned his appreciation.

He *had* to see her face. Knew she'd look impossibly beautiful in that moment. And sure enough, she did. But her glazed eyes and slack jaw didn't last long.

Clearly not appreciating the interruption, she grimaced and pounded her fist against the mattress. "Don't stop, damn you."

He knew better than to do anything but comply, so he lowered his head and returned his attention to her clit. If he could, he'd wring out every ounce of pleasure possible from her oncoming orgasm, so he slid two fingers into her sex, in hopes of finding her G-spot.

She released a guttural cry, a sound that filled him with satisfaction. Maybe he hadn't hit the jackpot on his first try, but she'd reached another level, and that made him want to pound his chest.

He kept a relentless pace, stirred to action by the sounds she made. Her cries grew louder, until a soft suck of her nub caused her to buck against his mouth. "Oh, yes, Ethan. I'm coming. Please. Don't. Stop."

Stopping was the farthest thing from his mind. But when her thighs clamped the sides of his head, he knew pleasure would soon become pain, so he lifted his head and stared at her flushed face.

Her breathing slowed, and she blinked her eyes open.

His heart squeezed at the sight. "Hi."

"Hello, down there."

"I need to be inside you right now."

"Come on up," she said as she pulled him toward her chest.

He reached over, ripped open the condom box, and sheathed himself in record time. Then he rose on his forearms and guided his cock into her. Staring down at her, he took in everything: her full lips, her smoky eyes, and her dark hair fanned against the pillow. He'd never tire of the view. "Gracie."

She reached up and squeezed his shoulders, the fortunate effect of which was to press her breasts together. "Ethan."

Her voice trembled, and his heart nearly stopped. "Say that again, Gracie."

"Ethan."

Everything was exactly as it should have been. The knowledge that he wasn't holding anything back from her freed him. Gave him license to lose himself in her totally. He thrust into her, moving with an intensity that matched the need in her voice. Each time he slipped out and pushed back in, she rose to meet him, matching his thrusts with a roll of her hips.

He wouldn't last long. Nor had he expected to. He covered her mouth with his, and lowered his body against hers. His muscles ached from the tension of being on the brink of orgasm. And when the orgasm finally slammed into him, he curled his toes into the mattress and ground his body against her to ride out the wave. Her hands caressed his back, soothing him as he recovered and his vision cleared.

He pressed his face into her neck and breathed in her sweet scent. "I love you so damn much, Gracie."

"I love you, too, Nicholas Ethan Hill."

He wanted to worship her. Today. Tomorrow. Forever. He marveled at the chance she'd given him. And he made a vow to spend the rest of his days making sure she'd never regret it.

Look for the next book in Mia Sosa's The Suits
Undone series, available in May 2016!

A preview follows.

CHAPTER ONE

The skin on the back of Karen Ramirez's neck prickled, warning her of the ambush a second before it happened. Before she could do anything about it, her older sister, Gracie, thrust a tumbler in her hand. "Swallow it."

Her sister's best friend, Mimi, erupted into a high-pitched cackle. "That's what he said." The petite blonde donned a coquettish smile and swayed to the music blasting through the club's speakers.

Karen gripped the heavy base of the whiskey glass and lifted the drink to her lips, buoyed by the steady beat of the unfamiliar pop song vibrating around her. Having chained herself to the desk in her dorm room for the last four years, she had no clue what to make of the song or the strobe lights flashing through the upscale club in D.C.'s Georgetown neighborhood. It all seemed…a bit much.

She pursed her mouth in distaste at the offending liquid and stared at Gracie with pleading eyes. When that didn't work, she shook her head in tepid refusal.

"It's whiskey, not mouthwash," Mimi pointed out. "Stop swishing it around in your mouth like that."

Okay, might as well get this over with. Karen gulped a generous amount of the honey-colored liquid and thumped a fist over her heart as the burn sped down her chest and settled in her stomach. Disgusting. People drank that crap on purpose?

Gracie, radiant as usual in a sleek black dress, patted Karen's back and smiled. "C'mon, Karen. Relax. It's not every day a Ramirez woman graduates from college. The books will be there in the morning." Gracie swept her arms in the direction of the dance floor. "For tonight, you need to let loose. Throw caution to the wind."

"Release your inner hussy and screw a hot man," Mimi added as she handed Karen more whiskey, this time in a shot glass.

Gracie's smile faded and she pinned Mimi with a warning stare. "Whoa there, partner. Rein it in. This is my baby sis you're talking to."

Mimi refused to shrink away. "Your *baby sis* is an adult. And she's entitled to sex, too, Ms. Getting-It-Every-Day-and-Making-the-Rest-of-Us-Jealous."

Gracie covered her ears. "La, la, la. Next subject, please."

Karen waved a hand in front of the dynamic duo. "Hello? I'm here, you know." She tipped back her head and took another shot. Good lord. Would she grow hair on her chest tonight, too?

Gracie dropped her hands and gave her sister a sheepish grin. "Sorry, Kar. Anyway, let's find a spot on the dance floor. I want to dance before Ethan gets here."

Karen didn't know her sister's boyfriend well; she'd been too busy at school to get to know him. But if he had a possessive streak, she and Gracie would have a talk—and then she'd be calling her male cousins in New York to have a "talk" with him.

Karen drew her sister to her side. "Why the rush? He doesn't like you to dance?"

Gracie shook her head. "No, nothing like that. The man has two left feet. I'm saving myself from the embarrassment."

Relieved, Karen took a last shot of whiskey—it went down easier the third time around—and let Gracie lead her to the dance floor, where Mimi had already managed to draw a semicircle of men around her.

Karen's heart rate quickened as strangers' bodies pressed against her. For someone who relished her personal space, this setting was less than ideal. Still, Gracie and Mimi were right. It wouldn't hurt to celebrate a little before she buckled down for the road ahead. Four years of medical school. Four years during which she'd have no time for distractions. Tonight, though, she could afford to throw caution to the wind. How much trouble could she get into with her sister in tow anyway?

* * *

Karen groped the wall and tried not to trip as she made her way to the ladies' room. Did the hall have to be so freakin' dark? She pressed her face against the velvet-covered wall, sighing when the soft fabric touched her cheek. Mmmm. Nice.

Speaking of which, whiskey was nice. She'd unfairly maligned the drink before experiencing the heady warmth that spiraled in her belly and radiated out to her limbs. Unfortunately, though, the whiskey also affected her in other, less welcome ways. Every step took more effort than she had energy for, like she was swimming in a giant vat of chewing gum. And a sheen of perspiration coated her arms. But she'd convinced Gracie that she was sober enough to get to the restroom, and she was determined to get there. Otherwise, she'd pee on herself in this swank club.

A few minutes later, after pressing a cool, wet cloth to her forehead and reapplying her lipstick, Karen left the ladies' room and slammed into a wall. Of chest. She sniffed the dress shirt that covered said chest and grinned. A woodsy scent with a hint of citrus filled her nostrils. Everything was so damn *nice* in this club.

She might have hummed her approval. *Maybe.* And the ensuing silence forced her to realize what she was doing. "You're going to be a gentleman and pretend I didn't sniff you, right?"

Strong hands helped her to remain upright. "Sure. You okay down there?"

The man with the baritone voice didn't bother to hide his amusement with her predicament. She lifted her head, wanting desperately to meet the owner of that voice. And sure enough, the owner did not disappoint. What she could see of him, at least.

Dark hair. Dark eyes. Devilish smile. That smile made her want to run, but she held her ground, because if she didn't, she'd topple over in the stilettos Gracie had persuaded her to wear.

She drew back a bit to survey him and experienced an inexplicable urge to snuggle into his massive chest. The shadows across his face highlighted certain traits and hinted at others: strong jaw, angular cheekbones, and hair that flopped carelessly over one eyebrow. He'd asked her a question, but she struggled to remember it. Something about whether she was okay, maybe?

Regaining her senses, she stepped out of his loose grasp. "Sorry about that. I'm fine. A celebration gone amuck. The uninitiated should never drink whiskey for the first time in a public place."

"Congratulations on whatever you're celebrating. It looks good on you. You're glowing."

Karen's cheeks warmed. She hoped she wasn't blushing. That would be embarrassing. Hell. Who was she kidding? This encounter had passed *embarrassing* and landed directly on *awkwardly humiliating* when she'd sniffed his shirt. Nevertheless, she managed to thank him, though her voice barely rose above a murmur.

Of its own volition, her body drifted closer to him.

His eyes, attentive to her every move, narrowed as she came closer. "Are you here alone?"

She must have frowned at the question, because he tripped over himself to explain.

"I'm not trying to pick you up," he said as he raised both hands in the air. "I promise. I don't generally cruise clubs for women."

Karen focused on the one word that held her interest. "Generally?"

His head lifted just a fraction, as though he himself were surprised by his use of the word. "No, not generally. I was asking because your . . . celebration might have affected your faculties, and I'd be an asshat if I didn't make sure you were safe before I left you."

She didn't bother to disagree with his assessment of her faculties, though, in truth, the whiskey hadn't decimated her senses.

"That's sweet." She should have stopped there. Really, she should have. But the buzz from the whiskey propelled her to act in ways that were foreign to her, erasing the lines she typically didn't cross. "It's also disappointing. I had high hopes for you."

Had she said that out loud? Yes. She. Had. Karen laughed to cover her embarrassment, a weak sound that drifted in the air like a deflated balloon. Needing to move, she pressed her hand against the back of her neck and winced when a trickle of sweat made its way down her back. Whatever. Karen wanted to be daring for a change, sweaty or not. "That didn't come out right. What I meant is, it's a shame that you won't be making a move on me. I'd like you to."

There. She'd said it.

A gaggle of women chose that moment to stumble through the hall on their way to the restroom. He backed up, and when the women had passed, he directed his measured gaze from the top of her head to the toes that peeked out of her abominably painful shoes.

Now that they were separated by a few feet, she rushed to study him in his entirety. The business suit hugged his frame as though it had been tailored for him. And judging from its seemingly expensive fabric, it likely had been. Everything about him screamed serious, broody businessman, from the silk tie he hadn't bothered to loosen despite his relaxed surroundings, to the crease between his brows. That is, until you considered his hair, which appeared to follow the whim of his fingers, and the ghost of a smile that begged for someone to draw it out completely.

That smile brightened when she began to smooth her hands over the front of her dress.

He studied her face. "Nervous, are we?"

"Out of sorts is all."

"Then it's a good thing I won't be making a move on you, no?"

She didn't detect any censure in his tone, but his words reminded her she knew nothing about this man, and although she wasn't drunk, she wasn't one hundred percent lucid, either. "Thanks for the advice. You're absolutely right."

His eyes widened when he realized she planned to leave, and he reached for her hand. "No. Wait. Please."

She ignored his hand and moved toward the main area of the club. "I should head back. This isn't me at all."

"I can tell."

Karen stopped moving and turned to face him. "That obvious, huh?"

"It wasn't meant as an insult, if that's what you're thinking. Just an observation."

"I'm not a specimen in a petri dish, thank you."

His face fascinated her. Right now, it said, *I'm intrigued, but I'm not sure if I should engage.* She made a mental note to take advantage of that fact if she ever played strip poker with him. Without any prompting from her, his face would reveal the strength of his hand, and she'd have him naked in minutes. Karen fanned herself at the thought and noticed his eyes dart to her jiggling breasts.

He shook his head, as though he needed to clear it, and then his gaze swept across her face. "No, you're not a specimen in a petri dish. Far from it."

Thank goodness he hadn't focused on her breasts. Such blatant ogling would have garnered him a scowl and a first-class ticket to

Jerklandia. Plus, she worried her nipples would poke his eyes out. And why was she itchy all of a sudden? *For goodness' sake, Karen, focus.*

He held up his hands. "May I approach?"

She appreciated the question. Would have fled had he moved toward her without gauging her interest. But what was she doing? What did she expect to happen here if he came closer? And when would her sister come looking for her? Karen had been gone more than five minutes, and Gracie had promised to watch for her return. What good was a designated driver without a passenger?

Unsure of his intentions, she nevertheless nodded. But as he walked toward her, her protective instincts kicked in and she changed her mind. "Stop," she said as she raised her hand like a crossing guard.

He stopped mid-stride. "I just want to talk."

"Okay. Let's start with your name."

"Mark."

"Nice to meet you, Mark. I'm Karen. What do you want to talk about?"

"The things I'd do to you if I were free to. I find the idea of talking about them just as enticing as actually doing them."

She raised a single eyebrow and gave him a dubious look. "Really?"

He grinned. "No, not really. But under the circumstances, talking will have to do."

Spurred by his words alone, Karen's brain supplied a barrage of images of them "talking" through the night.

He moved closer, until his breath skated over her ear. "You like that idea, don't you?"

On shaky legs, she tried to suppress her laughter. Dammit. She had to be the most ticklish person ever. If it weren't for that ridiculous fact, the movement of his lips near her ear would have been hot. Instead, though, she struggled not to fall to the ground in a fit of giggles. "Yes, I like that idea a lot."

With a hint of a smile that emphasized the dimple in his chin, he reached for her hand. "Come with me?"

Um. Did he mean that literally? "Too soon, stranger. We just met."

This time, he rewarded her with a full-blown grin. "I meant follow me."

So she did what any smart woman with too much whiskey in her system would do. She nodded her assent. And then she followed him. Down the hall. Past the emergency exit. Into an alcove with two chairs and a cocktail table nestled between them.

He pointed to one of the chairs, his long, tan fingers catching her attention. "Join me?"

Karen checked the chair bottom for suspicious substances. Finding none, she dropped into it, and the ensuing relief to her feet reached orgasmic levels.

Mark waited until she was seated before he took the chair across from her. "Are your feet hurting?"

Ack. That moan hadn't just been in her head. "That's an understatement."

He shifted closer to the edge of his seat and held out his hands. "Let me see."

She wanted to accede to his request, but first she had to address her litany of concerns. Three weeks into her pedicure, her feet had seen better days. She was sure they were clean. But she'd been sweating. And what about her heels? She'd been known to do a wicked impression of a woman who kicked flour all day.

He chuckled. "Where did you go?"

"Go?"

"In your head. It's like I lost you for a minute."

Karen tilted her head and sighed. "You did. It's what I do. You could be the most fascinating person in the world, but I tend not to focus on any one thing for long."

"Must do wonders for a man's ego."

He didn't mean any harm. To do that, he would have to know about her past relationships with men—which of course, he didn't. Still, the remark stung, and even though she owed him nothing, she regretted the loss of concentration. She dropped her chin. "Sorry about that."

He reached over and lifted her chin. "Nothing to be sorry for. And if my comment hurt you, I'm the one who should apologize."

This was all getting a little too . . . deep. Fun. She was supposed to be having fun. "It's okay. I'm fine." To prove the truth of that statement, she edged closer to him and lifted her legs. "May I?"

"Yes, set them on my lap."

As she did so, he unbuttoned his suit jacket. She couldn't resist asking him about his choice of attire. "Do you always wear business suits when you're trolling for women?"

He flashed his killer grin. "First, as I said before, I don't troll."

"Generally."

With a quirk of his lips, he nodded and slipped off her shoes. "Yes, generally. And second, the answer to your question is no. I was dragged here by a friend, and before that I was at a business meeting."

He slid her bare feet along his lap, causing her ankles to press against his muscled thighs. That would have been enough to short-circuit her brain, but he had more in store for her. He ran his fingers down her lower legs and cupped her calves, squeezing them lightly before trailing his fingers down her shins. Next, he circled the tops of her feet with the tips of his fingers, their warmth relaxing her and making her go limp. He possessed magic hands. Smooth. Strong. He kneaded her soles with them, attending to her feet with a deliberateness that led her to envision his hands in more intimate places.

"Tell me what you like," he said.

Karen forced herself not to stutter. "Like?"

He continued to massage her toes. "Sexually."

She opened her mouth, but nothing came out.

"Don't stress. We're just talking. Titillating discussion without having to do the walk of shame in the morning. You liked that idea, remember?"

Yes, she liked the idea, but what could she say? Hell if she knew what she liked. No one had ever bothered to worry about her pleasure, and she'd been too chicken shit to tell them what turned her on. "I'm not sure."

His face blanched, and his hands stopped moving. "You've had sex before, right?"

Pfft. Of course she had. But the experiences hadn't been enough to shut off her brain and stop her from blurting out ill-conceived observations. "Yes, I have."

"Tell me. I know there's something you want to say."

"How can you tell?"

"You dip your head to one side and rest your chin on your

shoulder, like you want to bury your head in your own neck. You did it before."

Would it be so bad to share her tics with a complete stranger? One she'd never see again? "Well, the thing is, I tend to lose my concentration during sex, too." She shook her head, knowing she wasn't explaining herself well. "No. It's more like I tend to concentrate on the wrong things."

He adjusted his body in the armchair. "Give me an example."

Karen shifted her torso away from him and covered her face with her hands. "It's too embarrassing." She peeked through her fingers. "Wait. Are you a therapist or something?"

He lifted a dark brow and shook his head no. "Hardly. We're just talking. And then you'll go off to your life, and I'll go off to mine."

Right. Exactly. "Okay, here's an example. The guy says, 'You're so wet,' because, you know, they *all* say that, and then my brain takes over. I ask myself, 'Am I? Am I, really? Or are you too small? Because I have to say, you're starting to feel like a tampon.'"

He laughed. A deep, rich laugh that made her want to join him. Her first impression of him had been replaced by this one. He wasn't broody at all. A man who laughed like that, his neck stretched to reveal his Adam's apple and his eyes gleaming in appreciation, could never be broody. Thoughtful, yes. Broody? No.

"And I'll never forget the first time a guy went down on me. He lapped at me like a poodle drinking from a water bowl, and I shit you not, I mimicked his lapping noises with my own tongue. I didn't even know I was doing it until he lifted his head."

Mark's shoulders shook after she shared that tidbit.

"But that's not all," she continued. "Sometimes I forget that I'm not supposed to articulate my thoughts, or I zone out, and before I know what's happening, the guy, who is rightfully pissed or hurt, scrambles for the door." She removed her feet from his grasp and set them on the floor. Staring at her toes helped her avoid his gaze. "And I feel awful. No one should feel inadequate like that, but I can't seem to help myself. I'd love to be able to lose myself in the moment, but it's never happened." She shrugged her shoulders. "Someday, maybe."

She didn't know what reaction she'd get. Sympathy? Ridicule? Whatever she got, it wouldn't matter. This was about her, not him, because that was the point of catharsis, after all. But when she dared to peek at his face, she nearly fell back against the chair. Lust. There it was. It seeped out of his pores. Made his slack jaw sexy. Darkened his brown eyes to black. Made his big body move with each breath he took.

"Mark?"

When he finally spoke, his voice contained a hint of gravel, a rough sound that exposed how her words had affected him. "What you said just then. Wanting passion that would make you lose all thought and admitting you've never experienced it? That's like waving a flag at a bull. God, there's not much I wouldn't do to get you under me if that's what you craved. To get you to the point where all you could think about was me. Us. How we fit together. How we move together."

She wanted that, too. She hadn't realized how much until his words had mirrored her thoughts. She burned with the need, in fact. And she squirmed in a feeble attempt to disguise the heat that suffused her. But this was crazy. They'd just met. It *had* to be the whiskey. The craziness of the night.

Shit. Gracie. Her sister was probably searching for her now.

She stood up and held on to the chair as she slipped her shoes back on. "I've got to rejoin my group."

He remained seated, a telltale bulge in his crotch suggesting that standing at this juncture would be uncomfortable for him. "I'd ask for your last name, but I'm afraid if I knew it, I'd try to find you. And that's not what this is about." He paused. "Right?"

What she'd told him was mortifying, and despite her attraction to him, the knowledge that she'd never see him again would ensure she'd survive the embarrassment. She didn't think long about her answer. "Right. Thanks for the talk, and have a great life, Mark."

Her objective was simple: to infuse her stride with a dab of sexiness and a pinch of confidence. She planned to turn around and leave him with a decent memory of her, one in which she wasn't wobbling away on three-inch stilettos. But her sister's worried voice calling out her name rooted her to the spot.

And seconds later, Gracie skidded into her. "Jesus, Karen. You scared the shit out of me. I've been looking everywhere for you."

Still facing Mark, Karen twisted her head in her sister's direction. "You found me. I'm fine."

Gracie's eyes widened when she saw that Karen wasn't alone.

For the second time that night, a frisson of dread ran through her. Was that a hint of recognition in Gracie's eyes? No. Fucking. Way. She'd just had one of the most embarrassing conversations ever with a man she assumed would remain a stranger. Her sister's face, however, suggested that wasn't the case. Karen quite literally prayed she'd read Gracie wrong.

But crap on a crostini, Gracie's frown suddenly changed to a broad grin. "Mark? Is that you?"

About the Author

Mia Sosa was born and raised in New York. She attended the University of Pennsylvania, where she earned her bachelor's degree in communications and met her own romantic hero, her husband. She once dreamed of being a professional singer, but then she discovered she would have to perform on stage to realize that dream and decided to take the law school admissions test instead. A graduate of Yale Law School, Mia practiced First Amendment and media law in the nation's capital for ten years before returning to her creative roots. Now, she spends most of her days writing contemporary romances about smart women and the complicated men who love them. Okay, let's be real here: She wears PJs all day and watches more reality television than a network television censor—all in the name of research, of course. Mia lives in Maryland with her husband and two daughters and will forever be on the hunt for the perfect karaoke bar.

Learn more at:

www.MiaSosa.com

Twitter: @MiaSosaRomance

Facebook.com/miasosa.author

CPSIA information can be obtained
at www.ICGtesting.com
Printed in the USA
FFOW02n1023021215
19161FF

9 781455 568413